To
Enjoy the
adventure!
Janet Muirhead Hill

Other Books by Janet Muirhead Hill

Book 1 - *Miranda and Starlight* (2002)

Book 2 - *Starlight's Courage* (2002)

Book 3 - *Starlight, Star Bright* (2003)

Book 4 - *Starlight's Shooting Star* (2003)

Book 5 - *Starlight Shines for Miranda* (2004)

Book 6 - *Starlight Comes Home* (2004)

Danny's Dragon (2006) A story of heartache and healing

The Twins Trilogy:

Kyleah's Tree (2008)

Kendall's Storm (2011)

Kendall and Kyleah (2012)

The Body in the Freezer (2014) (Young Adult)

A note from the author

Writing Miranda is always easy. I can relate to her in so many ways. Writing Teddy has proven harder because I've never been an Apsaalooké (Crow) child. Not that I didn't dream of it. When I was very young, I often imagined running away and joining a tribe of Indians that I thought was just over the mountain. But that was the white-man version of "Indian"—the version I saw in old western movies, the version enacted in old poems, skits, and songs, the version that got it wrong. I hope to got it right.

I have a high regard for every First Nation tribe. I've learned a lot about Crow culture, and although I know I have much more to learn, I have attempted to portray it with accuracy and respect. I've read books and researched online, hoping to avoid offense. If I have failed, I hope readers will understand that I meant no dishonor. Please forgive my ignorance. I will keep reading, discussing, and learning. Knowledge leads to understanding and understanding leads to love.

"If you understand each other you will be kind to each other. Knowing a man well never leads to hate and almost always leads to love." — John Steinbeck

"I think it's impossible to really understand somebody, what they want, what they believe, and not love them the way they love themselves." — Orson Scott Card, *Ender's Game*

"If we were alike," Danny said slowly, "we wouldn't need a bridge, would we? A bridge is for when things don't meet up. It doesn't change what's on either side. It just connects them."

— Janet Muirhead Hill, *Danny's Dragon*

Understanding builds bridges. For more understanding, check out the resources in the back of this book. Sometimes we offend others only because of our ignorance. Education is the remedy .

The Horse and the Crow
A Miranda and Starlight Story

Janet Muirhead Hill

Raven Publishing, Inc
Norris, MT 59745

The Horse and the Crow: a Miranda and Starlight Story

Published by: Raven Publishing, Inc.
PO Box 2866, Norris, Montana 59745

Library of Congress Cataloging-in-Publication Data

Hill, Janet Muirhead.
The horse and the Crow : a Miranda and Starlight story / Janet Muirhead Hill.
pages cm
Summary: "Fourteen-year-old Miranda worked hard to get her parents permission to compete in the Crow Fair races in Montana, never dreaming the dangers and discoveries that would result"-- Provided by publisher.
ISBN 978-1-937849-27-6 (pbk. : alk. paper) -- ISBN 978-1-937849-28-3 (ebook)
[1. Horses--Fiction. 2. Crow Indians--Fiction. 3. Indians of North America--Montana--Fiction. 4. Mystery and detective stories.] I. Title.
PZ7.H552813Ho 2015
[Fic]--dc23

2015011644

Dedicated to the memory of my friend and mentor,
Florence Ore, editor at Raven Publishing, Inc.
Rest in peace, dear Florence. Your influence lives on.

Chapter One

Miranda Stevens, age fourteen going on thirty, as her dad liked to say, had everything her heart could possibly desire. So why wasn't she the happiest girl on earth?

"I should be so excited about this weekend I'd be bouncing out of my boots," she said to the freckle-faced, green-eyed girl in the mirror. "So what is this feeling of —I don't know, dread? Fear? Like the world's coming to an end and I'm the only one who knows it? Only I don't know. It's just this feeling that something is wrong."

"Miranda, phone," Mom called, tapping on the bathroom door. "It's Laurie."

Miranda smiled. If anyone could cheer her up, her best friend could. But when she heard Laurie's voice, she asked. "You okay? Sounds like you have a bad cold."

"No," Laurie's voice caught in a sob. "I've been crying for the last hour."

"Why? What's wrong?" Miranda asked in alarm.

"I can't go. We're going to Cincinnati."

"What? Why?"

"My grandparents were in an accident. Papa's dead." Laurie began sobbing. Miranda waited. "Gram's in bad shape. I just can't believe I won't see Papa again. What if they both die before we get there?"

"Oh, Laurie, I'm so sorry." Miranda wanted to hug

her friend and cry along with her. She knew how she'd feel if anything happened to her grandparents. "When are you leaving? Can I come see you before you go?"

"No, we're leaving right now. We're driving. It's a long trip, but we couldn't get plane tickets except standby. Dad would rather drive than wait."

"Okay. I'll be thinking about you. Please call me when you get there."

"Yeah. I'll call your cell. You'll be in Crow Agency by then."

"Take care! I love you," Miranda said, wishing she could do more to comfort her friend.

Will I be in Crow Agency? I don't know how, she thought as she clicked off the phone. Laurie's parents had planned to take her, Laurie, Chris, and four horses to the annual Crow Fair in Crow Agency, Montana, the capital of the Crow Indian Reservation. They'd planned to leave tomorrow. She thought of how hard she'd worked to get permission to go. What if a little thing like no transportation stopped her now?

Miranda had wanted to go to the Crow Fair ever since she first heard of it at a school assembly last April. Her school had hosted a talk, "Native Americans in the Modern World" by a Crow woman named Mary Little Foot. She was married to Lisa's uncle Lyle, who didn't have an ounce of Indian blood, but seemed to embrace the culture as his own. When Lisa, a classmate of Miranda's, mentioned her Native American aunt, the social studies teacher was immediately interested and invited her to come speak to the class. Lisa didn't seem nearly as excited about that as Miranda was. When Miranda asked her why, Lisa shrugged.

"Well, Uncle Lyle isn't exactly someone we brag about in our family."

"Why?"

"Well, you know, no one thought he should marry someone like Mary."

"What's the matter with Mary?"

"Oh, nothing. It's just, you know, being from a different culture and all."

"You don't like him because he married a Crow woman?" Miranda was astonished.

"Well, it wouldn't be so bad if she'd at least taken his name. But, no. He wanted to take hers. He calls himself Lyle Little Foot, but I don't think it's legal."

From the time Miranda had come to Country View School at the end of fourth grade, she'd called the other girls in her class the "Magnificent Four," not because she thought they were magnificent, but because they acted as if *they* thought they were. When Laurie, who was part African American, joined their class the "MF" wanted nothing to do with her. That was okay with Miranda, because Laurie had quickly become her best friend.

Miranda and Laurie had eventually made friends of sorts with the Magnificent Four, as they were thrown together for various class projects and outings, but they were never close. Stephanie, Kimberly, Lisa, and Tammy did everything together. Miranda and Laurie didn't have much in common with them. Once again, Miranda understood why.

"I'd be thrilled if she was my aunt," Miranda had said about Mary Little Foot.

"I suppose you would," Lisa retorted, as if that were an insult. Then she hurried away to join Stephanie.

Mary had talked about the history of her people and the struggle to keep the young people interested in the traditions of the Crow people. The Crow Fair, held annually in Crow Agency, Montana, was a big factor in holding the interest of the Crow children. It was the biggest Native-American fair in the country and people from many tribes came to be part of it. People of all ages participated. Mary's slide show of the various events showed the colorful traditional clothing worn by people of all ages, from tiny toddlers to old men and women. The parades and the dances looked exciting and fun, but it was the horse races that interested Miranda the most.

"Could I enter my horse in the races?" Miranda had asked Mary after the assembly.

"Possibly. I'm sure I could find one of my neighbors who would be glad to ride it for you."

"No, I mean could I ride my horses in the fair. I'm the only one who can ride them."

"I'm afraid not, dear. And I'm sorry, but you have to be a tribal member in order to compete."

"I'd have to be Crow?"

"No, not since they changed the rules back in the 50s or 60s. It used to be that only Crows were allowed. Now, they let members of other tribes participate, too."

When Miranda had gone home that afternoon,

complained to her parents that she wished she'd been born Native American.

"Why?" her mom had asked.

"Because they are beautiful people," Miranda said, "and so I could race my horses at the Crow Fair."

"I guess I never told you that you are part Cherokee," Dad said.

"What? I am?"

"It just never came up. My great-grandmother was a full-blood Cherokee. But her husband was white, so my grandmother was only half-blood. She married a white man, making my father one-fourth blood and me just one-eighth. That makes you one-sixteenth Cherokee, enough to get tribal membership, if you wanted it. It never occurred to me that you would. I never got around to getting membership myself. My father died when I was ten, and mom and I went to live with her Norwegian parents in Iowa. I grew up there, and no one ever suggested that I should get tribal membership."

"Did you ever go visit your grandmother? The Indian one?"

"No. I knew that she lived in North Carolina with that branch of the Cherokees, but my mom was not a very healthy person. We never traveled."

"Oh, I wish I could have known her—my great grandmother, I mean. Is she still alive?"

"I don't think so. She'd be very old by now." Dad looked a little sad. "I used to get a present in the mail on my birthday when I was little, but they stopped coming when I was twelve or thirteen. And, as I'm sure you know, my mother died several years ago, and her parents were gone before that."

"How sad!" Miranda felt as if a huge part of her life was swept away as soon as she knew about it. If only she could have been a part of that side of her family! But, she reminded herself, the good news was that she was part Native American. "Can we start now? Start getting us registered, so I can enter the races and stuff?"

"Hey, no one has said you could go, no matter what the Crow Fair officials say," Mom said.

"I know. You and Dad still have to talk about it. But think what an opportunity it is for me to learn about my heritage. Because, even if I don't get to go, I want to be able to say that I'm Cherokee and start learning more about what that means."

Mom had agreed that it was a good idea to establish her tribal membership if she could. "We should do that for Kaden, too." Kaden was Miranda's youngest brother, the only kid in the family besides herself who wasn't adopted. "I think it's important to know one's genealogy, so go ahead. But," her mother had warned, "don't think that means you are going to the fair."

The first step had been to prove her father's lineage, which turned out to be far easier than Miranda had expected. With Dad busy with his work and taking care of the ranch, he left it up to Miranda to do the research and file the needed paperwork. Miranda was busy, too, with school, her chores, and her horses. She made sure she spent at least a little time each day working with Shooting Star, her two-year-old filly, to be sure she was ready for the fair. When she finally researched the Eastern Band of Cherokee rolls, she learned that not only her great-great grandmother and her father's grandmother and his father, but even Dad were registered members of the tribe.

Dad was surprised to learn this. He seemed ashamed that he hadn't kept in touch with his father's relatives. "My grandma must have really cared about me, even though I never knew her."

Miranda filled out the application for her own membership, had her father sign it, and sent it in. When she received a letter back from them, she opened it eagerly. To her dismay, it was not her certificate of membership, but a letter saying she'd have to wait until she was eighteen to reapply. *At this time, we are only extending memberships to infants and to teenagers when they turn eighteen.*

Miranda, once she got over the bitter disappointment that she felt initially, convinced herself that it didn't matter. All she had to do was to take her father's tribal membership card, which had already come in the mail, and her birth certificate, and it would prove that she was one-sixteenth Cherokee. The requirements for membership, besides what to her was a silly age restriction, was that she was at least one-sixteenth Cherokee blood and that a direct ancestor was listed on the 1924 Baker Roll, records that dated back to 1835 and listed all the Eastern Cherokee within the limits of North Carolina, Tennessee, Georgia, and Alabama. At least two of hers were on that list.

Miranda had kept in touch with Mary Little Foot ever since she'd met her at the school assembly. Mary was very helpful, and they'd become friends. Mary even invited Miranda and Laurie to camp with them at the fair. It was one thing that helped persuade Mom to let them go. She'd be with the Little Foots and Laurie's parents, Preston and Sheree Langley.

But now, the Langleys wouldn't be there. Not only was Miranda full of sadness and concern for her best friend, but she was very worried about what this news would do to her plans to go to the fair.

"Well, I'm not going to let it stop me!" she said to no one.

Chapter Two

She punched in the Bergman's phone number and asked to speak to Chris, her second best friend. At least that's what she always told herself, though it was pretty much a toss up between him and Laurie.

Christopher Bergman had started out to be her worst enemy when she was in fourth and fifth grades, but ended up as a friend and ally—until he kissed her a few months ago. She kind of wished the kiss had never happened because the feelings it evoked confused her. Even though the memory of it thrilled her, she had seen too many kids fall in love and then break up and never speak to each other again. She valued Chris's friendship too much to risk losing it, so she did her best to maintain the more comfortable camaraderie they'd had before the kiss had sent an unfamiliar shock wave through her.

"He's on his way to your house, Miranda." Mrs. Bergman said, "He got his license today."

"Oh, good, I'll..."

Before she could finish, Mrs. Bergman interrupted. "But he can't take you for a ride. His dad and I told him he's not allowed to drive with minors in the car unless there is an adult in the passenger seat."

"Okay, I think he's here. Bye." Miranda clicked off the phone and ran outside.

"Hey, Miranda. I'm legal now. Wanna go for a ride?"

"Yes, but not in your truck. I just talked to your mom and she warned me..."

"What? She called? She apparently doesn't trust me, does she?" Chris sounded indignant, and Miranda laughed.

"And obviously for good reason, huh?"

"I was going to stay on the back roads," Chris said, shrugging.

"Well, I have a better idea. Actually, I called your house, not vice versa."

"Why?"

"To see if you could come over. I have terrible news. We need to talk."

"What news? Talk about what?"

"Not here. Let's saddle up and ride over to see Higgins. We can talk on the way."

"All right, but Queen might be in season..."

Chris and Miranda had learned the hard way that it was not a good idea to take Chris's mare and Miranda's stallion, Starlight, out together when Queen was in her estrous cycle. Shooting Star was the only good result of that disastrous day.

"It's okay, I'm riding Star."

"Shooting Star?" Chris sounded wary.

"Of course, unless you want to ride her."

"No way! She's still a bit too frisky for my taste. You'll make her behave, right?"

"Sure. Don't I always?"

"No," Chris began, but Miranda was running toward

the house, calling over her shoulder, "I'm getting some cookies to take to Higgins. Meet you at the barn."

As they rode through the river pastures between her house and the old Caruthers' place where Higgins lived, Miranda told Chris all about Laurie's sad news. "Poor Laurie. Her heart is broken, and there is nothing I can do about it." After a pause, she added, "Now we don't have a way to get to the Crow Fair."

"Bummer! That's terrible about Laurie," Chris said. "Too bad about the fair, too. I know how much you've been looking forward to racing Starlight again."

"Ever since I found out that I'm part Cherokee, I've done everything to get permission to go. I never gave up getting the paperwork so I could get in. Then convincing Mom to let me enter was the hardest part. She finally came around when the Langleys were so excited about going. But I'm not giving up now."

"Of course not," Chris grinned at her.

"How about your folks. Would they reconsider?"

"No way. Dad has to run the store because his help is on vacation, and Mom has a party Saturday."

As president of the garden club, a member of the bridge club, and a cosmetic consultant, Mrs. Bergman was always having a party—or so it seemed to Miranda.

"Talk your parents into it," Chris said, "or your grandparents,"

"I've tried, Chris. Gram and Grandpa are in Kalispell, helping with my new baby cousin, and Mom has been against the idea from the beginning. If I mention this to her, she won't let me go."

"Why, exactly, doesn't she want you to go?"

"It's the racing part she objects to. She has the silly idea that I'm going to get hurt or killed somehow."

"Geez, I wonder why?" Chris grinned at his sarcasm. Miranda chose to ignore it.

"I think she's kind of mad at Dad for talking her into letting me go. If it weren't for him and the Langleys saying it would be a good cultural experience, I wouldn't have a chance."

Chris didn't seem as disappointed as she was, so she added, "Aren't you excited about going? There'll be so much to see, including your mare winning a race."

"I'm not sure how you talked me into letting you ride Queen in one of the races. You don't know if she'll win. Don't you think Indians have fast horses and know how to ride them?"

"I didn't say they didn't; in fact I'm sure they do. I just think our horses are tops."

"Maybe I won't mind seeing you lose a race or two. Maybe then you'll be ready to just have fun riding and taking care of them without risking your life."

"Racing is so much fun, and Queen'll do fine. But the important one is Star. I've got to race her, and this is the only chance. We'll be back in school before the race in Billings. Mom sure isn't going to let me skip school for a horse race."

"Why is it so important to race Shooting Star?"

"She's at her prime right now. I want to show my parents what she can do so they'll let me enter her in more races before she's too old."

"Yeah, she's all of two. Better hurry before she dies of old age." Chris could be so sarcastic. Miranda felt like punching him.

"In the big races like the Kentucky Derby, only two- and three-year-olds run."

"The Derby? Seriously, Miranda?" Chris mocked.

"No, I'll never get to race her in the big ones," Miranda said with her fingers crossed. "If Mr. Taylor were still here, I bet he'd make it happen."

Chris grinned at her and teased, "You'd fall off, and she'd lose, so I guess it's just as well."

"I don't fall off!" Miranda exclaimed. "And I think she's as fast as Starlight, if not a little faster. We ought to race them before we go. You can ride Shooting Star, and I'll ride Starlight." No one but Miranda rode Starlight.

"No, thank you! I'll stick with Queen. I'm comfortable with her."

They rode in silence for a couple of minutes.

"Miranda, I can see where your Mom's coming from. Star is skittish. I hope she doesn't blow up on you when she's in the middle of all the activity and noise. All the horses and people. She'll find plenty to freak out about."

"You'll behave just fine, won't you, baby girl?" Miranda said, patting Shooting Star's neck. The words were barely out of her mouth when a rabbit jumped up from under the horses' noses and darted away. Shooting Star leapt sideways and took off running.

Miranda grabbed leather for just a second and tightened her legs to stay in the saddle. Securing her seat quickly, she fought for control of the filly.

"Whoa! Not like that, you imp," Miranda said, reining her in and trotting back to Chris.

Queen looked sideways at her daughter. Miranda laughed. "Look at Queen. She's saying, "What's the matter with you, child? Scared of a little bunny?"

"Miranda, you dork. That's just what I'm scared will happen at the race, only worse."

"I didn't fall off, did I?"

"Not this time."

"Chris, we're going to the fair. We've just got to figure out how."

"Just wait for another race. Maybe Shooting Star will be a little calmer by then."

"No!"

"Then get your dad to take us."

"He can't. He promised to finish building that house for the principal, and he has a deadline. He's working long hours and weekends to get it done. Besides, Mom's already mad at him for talking her into letting me go. I hate being the cause of an argument between them."

"Too bad Mom and Dad won't let me drive without an adult along. I know I could handle the horse trailer."

"Yeah, I know. But even if they would, Mom would never let me go without a grownup with us the whole time." Miranda jumped off her horse to open the gate that led into the barnyard. "Let's put the horses in the barn and go talk to Higgins."

As she unbridled Star, put a halter on her, and loosened the cinch, Miranda thought about how much had changed since she'd first met Higgins nearly five years ago. She was in fifth grade, living with her grandparents on their dairy while her mother looked for work as an actress in California. She hadn't known a thing about her father at the time. Chris was still "her worst enemy," but she'd gone to Shady Hills Horse Ranch with him to see his new mare—and found the horse of her dreams, Starlight. Higgins worked there as the groom and horse trainer. Miranda had run to him for help when Starlight fell into a bog and got tangled in barb wire—after she'd let tried to ride the young black stallion and accidentally let him out of his paddock.

Higgins had seemed old even then, but he and Miranda had become close friends as she continued to visit Starlight and help him back to health. Since then, Mom had come back from California and adopted a toddler named Kort—and almost married a man that Miranda hated. That was how Margot came into their lives. Instead, of marrying the man, Mom had ended up adopting his daughter, giving Miranda a sister who was four years younger than she was.

It had been a close call. Wedding plans were in the making when Dad showed up. Everyone had thought he was dead. He and Mom renewed their wedding vows and built a house right there on Grandpa's dairy so that Miranda had all of her loved ones nearby. She had lived with her grandparents, John and Kathy Greene for so long, she didn't think she could be happy without seeing them every day.

A year later, baby Kaden was born, increasing their family to four kids where she'd been the only one such a short time before. But that wasn't the end of it. When the Cash Taylor, the Shady Hills Ranch owner, died, his grandson, Elliot, who was Margot's age, came to live with them, too.

Mr. Taylor had been more than an employer to Higgins. He'd been his best friend since childhood. When he passed away and Shady Hills was sold, Higgins no longer had a place to live. But things worked out, for not long before that, a ranch that bordered Grandpa's property had come up for sale. Dad bought it from a man named Caruthers. The house on the new property was small and vacant, so Dad asked Higgins to live there and work for him as caretaker. It was perfect.

The other perfect part came when Grandpa and Grandma sold their milk cows and Dad turned the old dairy barn into a horse stable. After Mr. Taylor's death, all of horses that belonged to Chris, Laurie, Margot, Elliot, and Miranda, including three that Mr. Taylor willed to her, came to live on the Stevens/Greene Ranch. That included the section of land that was Grandpa's and the two sections that Dad had bought from Mr. Caruthers. Miranda and her friends called the whole spread, "Heavenly Acres."

Higgins, short, bowlegged, and bright-eyed, met them on the back veranda.

"Well, well. My favorite horse ranchers. Good to see you."

Miranda gave him the bag of cookies and a kiss on the cheek. "Sorry the cookies are so crumbled. They got jostled a bit when Star saw a rabbit."

Higgins laughed. "They'll taste just as good in pieces as they would whole. Saves me from breaking them up when I soak them in my coffee." He took the cookies inside and invited Chris and Miranda to follow. "What brings you here, anyway? I figured you'd be busy getting ready to head to Crow Country. Yet, you took time for an old man—and to bake cookies, even."

"I always have time for a friend," Miranda said, "and I didn't bake. Margot did."

"And?" Higgins asked, his blue eyes twinkling.

Miranda grinned. No sense in pretending. Higgins had always been able to read her most secret thoughts. "Higgins, how would you like to go with us?"

"Why, I'd love to tag along, but I'm not up to driving that far anymore, and I don't think you have room for me in the truck."

"But we do now. Laurie and her parents can't come." Miranda filled Higgins in on the sad news about Laurie's grandparents. "So, it will just be you and Chris and me."

"I got my driver's license this morning, so I can do the driving," Chris said.

"Hmm, so what you really need is a chaperon so your folks will let you go."

Miranda smiled sheepishly and nodded. "Will you?"

"As long as this young whippersnapper lets me take a turn or two at the wheel," Higgins said squinting in Chris's direction.

"Sure. If you want to," Chris agreed.

"And," Higgins added, puffing out his chest, "Let me instruct you on your driving any time I feel it's called for. Without you taking any offense."

Chris groaned. "Okay, give me all the back-seat advice you want as long as you don't squeal and yell like Mom does."

"So when do we leave? Friday?" Higgins asked.

"No, tomorrow—Wednesday. I want to get there in time to sign up for the races I plan to enter. Lisa's aunt will be setting up her tipi in the afternoon. We can get the horses settled and be all ready for when the first session of the powwow that starts on Thursday." When Higgins didn't answer right away, Miranda asked, "You can go tomorrow, can't you?"

"I'll be ready."

Chapter Three

As Miranda expected, Mom raised all kinds of objections while Dad sat quietly and listened.

"I finally agreed to let you go because there would be two adults along to keep track of you. I know what happens when I send my daughter off with an old man who has no experience with children." Mom was referring to the time she let Miranda go to Texas with Mr. Taylor. He'd let her ride in a professional horse race—posing as a man.

"We're not children," Miranda said.

"No, you're teenagers, and that's worse."

"You mean you don't trust us?"

"No, I don't mean that. I mean you need guidance."

"Chris and I are both responsible."

"You are impulsive, and Christopher will go along with any harebrained idea you get. And as a driver, he's inexperienced. Didn't he just get his license? And a restricted one at that?"

"Mom, he's a great driver. He learned to drive long before we took driver's ed, and he's had a learner's permit for at least six months. Do you know what the instructor said about Chris and me? He said, 'I guess the only reason you two took this class is so you can get your driver's licenses when you turn fifteen.' He said that because we were already accomplished drivers. That's the word he used—accomplished."

"Maybe so, but he hasn't had much experience on the interstate or in town—or pulling a trailer."

"Yes, he does. We drove on the interstate and in Bozeman and Butte when we took driver's ed. He did just fine."

"And I've seen him back a trailer up to the dock at the store. He did that just fine, too," Dad put in.

Mom shot Dad a withering look and directed the next words at him. "These are just kids. They need adult supervision. Higgins is a dear, but he's old. His eyes are probably failing him, and I know his hearing isn't what it used to be."

"Higgins and I were out in the pasture checking fence this spring. He spotted a new fawn, a coyote, and a pair of sandhill cranes well before I could make them out. That man has eagle eyes." Dad wasn't paying attention to Mom's warning glares. Miranda loved that he was sticking up for her but was scared that it would cause hard feelings between her parents.

"So, I suppose you think we should let her go," Mom said in a tone of voice that indicated that she did not agree.

"I don't see why not since we already said she could. If I were looking for a responsible adult to look after my kids, I don't think I'd find anyone I'd trust more than Higgins."

"Mom, aren't you forgetting that I'll be staying with Lisa's aunt and uncle? They're grownups."

"Grownups that I've never met. And they haven't agreed to take responsibility or watch you every minute. I'm sure they have a lot of other things to do."

"You think I have to be watched every minute?" Miranda asked, indignantly.

"We don't watch her every minute when she's home," Dad said. "You must admit, she's been very dependable lately."

Mom threw up her arms and said, "Fine. Just remember, if anything goes wrong, it wasn't me who thought it was a good idea."

Higgins arrived early in the morning just as Chris backed the truck up to the gooseneck trailer, lining up the hitch perfectly on the first try. The four-horse trailer had living quarters in front. When all the wires and chains were properly connected, Miranda loaded the horses, putting Queen and Shooting Star in the front and closing the center gate. She tied Starlight behind Queen, leaving one empty stall. She went back and patted Lady's face as she nickered to the others. Sorry, but you can't go. I'd like to take you, but I can't without Laurie. It wouldn't be right. I'll bring your buddies back safely, I promise." She said it with complete confidence that she'd be able to keep her word.

Soon they were on the road, Chris driving the crew cab truck, Higgins riding shotgun, and Miranda hunched forward in the back seat. She frowned as she stared at the road ahead. The feeling she'd had the morning before was back, full force—an overwhelming sense of doom. Now, where the heck was that coming from?

Miranda leaned back and closed her eyes, trying to sort out the feeling that wouldn't go away. It wasn't like her to worry. Besides, she wasn't worrying about any one thing or problem. Whatever it was had no face or name, just a feeling—a premonition. Maybe that was it. She thought about Laurie and her heart ached for her friend. What if something like that happened to Grandma and Grandpa on their way home from Kalispell? What if a drunk driver came around a corner on their side of the road? *Now you're worrying, Miranda,* she chided herself. *Just stop it.* Maybe all of this foreboding was just the result of Laurie's news. Except, she remembered, she'd felt it before Laurie called.

The pickup rocked and jerked. Miranda's eyes flew open.

"Easy, boy!" Higgins exclaimed. "Better slow down a little."

"Sorry. Seemed like the trailer just pulled me the opposite way I was trying to go," Chris muttered.

"Well, you have it under control now," Higgins said.

"What happened?" Miranda asked as she tried to get her heart to slow down and quit banging the inside of her ribcage.

"Well, lead foot, here, thought he should pass that motor home—on a curve, no less. Fishtailed a bit and almost hit it."

Miranda noted Chris's white-knuckled grip on the steering wheel. She couldn't see his face, but his ears were red.

"Sensible lad that he is," Higgins said wryly, "he dropped back in and got behind it, and, if I'm not mistaken, he'll take it a little slower from here on out."

Miranda watched the motor home ahead of them and saw that it was going slower as it climbed a hill.

"Can I pass now?" Chris asked.

"Just stay behind. You've got a load, too, so you won't be able to go as fast as you think you can going up that grade," Higgins said. "Besides, I'd like for you to pull into that rest area at the top of the hill."

Chris did as Higgins asked, turning in and stopping without any more jerks or swerves. As Higgins got out, he said, "You two unload the horses while we're here. Let them stretch their legs."

By the time Higgins was back from the restroom, all three horses were out of the trailer. Higgins stroked each one and examined their legs and hooves. Patting Shooting Star, he said, "Now load them up. Put Queen in the same spot and Starlight in the front next to her. Shooting Star can go in behind her momma."

"I get it," Miranda said. "Even out the weight. Starlight's the heaviest, and Shooting Star's the lightest. That way the trailer's more balanced."

Higgins grinned at her and nodded. He watched them load the horses. When the trailer gate was secure, he said, "If you don't mind, son, I'll drive for a while."

Chris looked relieved as he went around to the passenger side. "My turn to ride in front," Miranda said. Chris didn't argue, but crawled into the back seat. Higgins drove the rest of the way to Crow Agency.

When Miranda saw the sign for Crow Agency, she was disappointed that she didn't see all the tipis as they'd looked in pictures on the Internet. But, once they passed the grove of trees, exited I-90, and turned toward the town they came into view. "Tipi city! They weren't kidding!" she exclaimed.

Advertised as the "Tipi Capital of the World," the Crow Fair sported what the brochure said were 1500 tipis. Mary Little Foot had told her that might be an exaggeration, but there were probably more than a thousand, plus a lot of tents and some campers. Seeing them was even more impressive than reading the numbers. Mary had also told her that the word for the Fair: Chichi-a'xxaawasuua in the Crow language means "running in circles."

It was established in the early 1900s by the federal government in consultation with the Crow people to promote farming practices, raising crops and farm animals, much like the white man's county fairs. Miranda had felt a stab of injustice when Mary said, "This was after the government had killed off the great buffalo herds."

Miranda had felt ashamed to be part of a culture that would wipe out the Crows' livelihood, lifestyle, and traditions so they could replace them with their own. How arrogant! She was glad to hear that the Crow Fair had grown to become a celebration of native traditions and history.

Miranda couldn't help but stare at the sights and whirl of activity as Higgins pulled into the fairgrounds and asked directions. Mary Little Foot had reserved a spot for her tipi next to the Little Big Horn River that ran through the town. She had told Miranda there would be room for them to park their trailer/camper next to it. Mary had planned for Laurie, Miranda, and Mrs. Langley to sleep in her tipi. Chris and Mr. Langley would sleep in the trailer. Seeing the Little Foot's lodge made her miss Laurie more than ever.

There was a small corral on the other side of the tipi. When the horses were settled in with the Little Foot's horses and given some hay to keep them content, Miranda asked Chris if he wanted to go with her to sign up for the races.

"If you can wait a bit. I'm helping Higgins get the trailer level, so we can sleep tonight."

"No, I'll go ahead, and then we can look around." Mary gave her directions and wished her luck.

"I'm here to sign up for the races. I have three horses, but I want to enter four races," Miranda said as she approached the desk and laid her paperwork in front of the man sitting there.

When he looked up at her, she noticed that he looked much younger than she'd first thought, not much older than she was. He frowned as he picked up the papers. "Cherokee?" he asked with disbelief in his voice. He studied her face, taking in her green eyes and dark blonde hair. He looked down at the papers and back at her. "You are not Barry Stevens. Do you have a membership card of your own?"

"Not yet. But Barry is my dad and so that makes me one-sixteenth Cherokee. My birth certificate proves it."

"I don't know. I'm new at this. I'll have to ask someone."

"But why? That other paper shows that my relatives are listed on the 1924 Baker Roll. I've highlighted the names. I will be a registered member as soon as I turn eighteen."

"I know nothing about Baker Rolls. I just need a certificate that says you are a tribe member. I'll have to ask my supervisor. Sorry."

"When will you know?"

"Come back tomorrow. He'll be here."

"But I might miss the first race I wanted to enter."

"There will be more like it the next day."

"But can't you find out today?" Miranda was aware that she sounded pushy, but she really wanted to race Shooting Star in the first race. She started to argue, but gave up with a shrug when he looked past her and said, "Next."

Miranda lay awake far into the night, enthralled with the many sounds: people moving around and voices gradually dying out. The drumming of horse hooves moving by on the hard packed earth was music to her ears. So were the twittering of night birds and the scurrying swish of small animals somewhere near. The river provided constant background music. She smiled, happy to be here with only a canvas wall between her and the natural world. She could even see the stars through the opening in the top of the tipi.

She felt like she was part of this new family. With the Crow people she'd met so far, she felt a kinship that made her wonder how strong the blood of her great, great-grandmother was. She was glad she was Native American, but she wished she were Crow, especially after her encounter with the young man who refused to let her sign up to be in the race.

She thought of her ancestors, wondering if they were at all like the Crow people who had roamed these very plains back in the days when wild buffalo were plentiful and life was simpler—*kind of like this is right now.* Miranda's thoughts kept wandering, imagining what it would be like to be a Native child back then. Nothing but horses for transportation. No cars, no Internet, or cellphones. Oops! She realized she'd forgotten to bring her cell phone. Oh well. She didn't think she'd miss it. She'd call Laurie as soon as she got home.

She realized that the feeling that something dire was about to happen was gone. She felt peaceful, and the feeling gave her complete confidence that the young man's supervisor would look over her papers and give her permission to race. She felt as if she was finally where she was meant to be. As her eyes grew heavy, she drifted into a dream world where horses danced, and the sound of their hoof beats and nickers soothed her.

Sounds of voices and the aroma of good things to eat awakened Miranda. Sunlight filled the opening in the tipi where she'd watched the stars last night. She jumped up and dressed quickly. Mary and Lyle were gone. She had meant to be up at dawn to tend to her horses, prepare everything for the race and the parade, and retrieve her paperwork and permission to race. The horses needed a good brushing, and she'd planned to braid Shooting Star's mane before the parade. Now, there was no time.

Chris came stumbling out of the camper, all sleepy-eyed, the same time she emerged from the tipi. Higgins sat in a canvas-folding chair, sipping a cup of coffee.

"Higgins, why didn't you wake me? I have a million things to do before the parade starts."

"Is that my job?" he asked, unabashed. "I'm sure you'll get done what needs doing. If you were sleeping that hard, it's because you needed the sleep. This will be a long day."

"I'm getting something to eat," Chris announced. "I'm starving."

"I'm checking on the horses," Miranda said. "I'll join you in a while if I get time."

"Don't you have a horse, too?" Higgins asked Chris.

Chris sighed. "Yeah. All right, Miranda, hold up. I'm coming with you."

"Hurry up then," Miranda called, trotting around the tipi to the small corral.

"Good morning, Queen," Chris said, patting his mare's nose and offering her a horse treat. Queen ate it and nuzzled his pocket for more.

Miranda greeted Starlight in much the same way. She loved that he always seemed eager to see her, whether she had a treat for him or not. She didn't this morning. She'd forgotten to fill her pockets in her rush. She petted the tall, black stallion's nose as she crooned to him about what a good boy he was and how much fun they were going to have today. "I'll lead you down to the river so you can get a drink. Then I'll come back and get your baby," she said, kissing his muzzle and buckling on his halter.

She followed Chris and Queen through the gate of the corral and carefully closed it behind them so that none of the other horses would get out. She stood mesmerized by the early morning sun reflecting off the waters of the Little Big Horn River as Starlight drank his fill. When Starlight finished she led him back, removed his halter, and called for her filly.

"Shooting Star? Where are you, baby girl? Are you mad at me for bringing you here? Come on." The red filly didn't come. Miranda searched among the other horses that shared the corral.

"Chris!" Miranda screamed after counting every horse. "Star's not here!"

Chapter Four

Miranda stared at Higgins, silently challenging him to take action. She wanted him to shout orders, move, get them organized in a search, anything, but he sat there all calm, doing nothing.

"I'm getting Starlight and going out to find her. I've done everything else I can think of," she said. "Chris and I searched everywhere around here. We asked everyone we met. No one knows where she could have gone."

"And where do you propose to find her on horseback?" Higgins asked. "There is a chance, though a small one, I think, that she was stolen. If so, she may be packed up in someone's trailer and out of state by now."

"I've thought of that, but what if someone took her and rode up into the hills somewhere?"

Chris interrupted. "We should report it to the cops if you think someone loaded her up and headed out. People have to stop at weigh stations if they're pulling a horse trailer, don't they? We did in Billings."

"We're supposed to stop with brand inspection papers and proof of a Coggins test. But if we'd gone on, it's likely that nothing would have come of it. Wyoming's the same. They might not go after a pickup and horse trailer."

"We can post her picture on the Internet. There are several places. But it hardly ever does any good," Miranda said with a sigh that was almost a sob.

"The parade is starting in fifteen minutes," Mary Little Foot announced as she led her horse from the corral. Both she and her horse were arrayed in beautiful Native dress. "Did you get signed in?"

"Mary, one of my horses is missing. I've got to find her before I do anything else. Can you tell me where she could have gone if she got out of the corrals? She could have crawled under the fence, I guess. It wouldn't be the first time."

"Your red filly?" Mary asked.

Miranda nodded as she fought the urge to cry.

"I'm so sorry," Mary said. "I wish I could help you find her, but I have to get to the parade lineup. I'll ask everyone I see if they've seen her. There are roads going both east and west. If she crossed the river and went under the interstate, she'd have to follow the highway. If she went east, she could fan out on miles of open land."

"She's been known to imitate Houdini," Chris interjected. "I bet she got out on her own and is grazing somewhere in that pasture land."

"Yeah," Miranda agreed. "She'd never cross the river or go under the highway. She's doesn't like water or traffic.

"Well, I hope you find her before the first session of the powwow begins at noon," Mary said.

When she had gone, Chris turned to Higgins. "I've got to help Miranda find Star. She's my horse, too."

"Now, don't you two go getting yourselves lost or hurt while I'm responsible for you. I'm not sure your parents would like you going off by yourselves."

"Higgins," Miranda said. "You know we do it all the time at home. Our parents let us. You can call them if it would make you feel better."

"Well, I just might do that. You kids be careful and be back before dark."

Miranda was taken aback by his quick acquiescence, giving them the whole day to search. "We'll head east. She's spooky about water, so I don't think she'd cross the river," she repeated, reassuring herself.

Chris, as usual, was thinking about food. "Start saddling up, Miranda. I'll fix some lunch to take along."

As they rode southeast toward low-lying brown hills, they kept their horses, Starlight and Queen, at a walk and watched for tracks in the dust.

"These hoof prints are about her size," Chris said as he stopped and stared at the ground.

Miranda urged Starlight to Queen's side. "Could be any horse. There are about a million here today."

"More or less." Chris laughed at her exaggeration. "But these are horseshoe prints. I don't think Indians shoe their horses."

"Of course, they do. As much as anyone, I bet. You've been watching too many old westerns." Miranda wasn't sure she was right.

"Have not. I read that somewhere." Chris sounded embarrassed and changed the subject. "We'd better hurry. Looks like a lot of country to cover before dark."

"True. But let's go slow enough to follow these tracks as long as we can see them."

"So, you agree it could be Shooting Star."

"Didn't say it couldn't," Miranda said. "I don't know whether Crow people shoe their horses or not. Maybe some do and some don't."

They rode in silence for a while, staring at the ground and trying to keep the hoof prints in view. The tracks soon disappeared in the hard, grassy ground. The two riders picked up the pace to a gentle trot as they followed a fairly straight line over the low hills.

As they crossed acres of treeless pasture land, Miranda noticed she was sweating more than her horse, though both horses were working up a lather under their headstalls and saddles. She estimated that it was close to a hundred degrees, maybe more. There had been no sign of a horse. She pulled Starlight to a halt.

"See those trees over there? Maybe there's water. Let's go sit in the shade and eat our lunch."

"Best idea you've had all day," Chris said, turning Queen toward a line of green in the distance.

It proved to be farther than it looked, and the stream was nothing more than a sandy bed with no water.

Miranda slid off Starlight and loosened his saddle. "Sorry, boy. I bet you're thirsty, and there's not a drop of water here." She stopped talking as her throat swelled and her lips began to quiver. She turned her back to Chris, not wanting him to see her cry.

"Well, dang!" Chris said. "The lunch is, uh, mush. Or

crumbles. But still edible, I guess." He plopped on the ground atop the saddle pad he'd just removed from Queen and took a bite of some nondescript tidbit he scooped from a plastic sandwich bag. "Yeah. Tastes just fine. Come have a bite, Miranda."

"You go ahead, I'm going to walk along this draw and see if there are any pools of water."

"Want me to come?"

"No. You stay. I need some privacy."

"Oh, sure. I'll try to save you some food."

Miranda left her horse and walked fast, fighting her frustration, replacing fear with anger. Fear that she'd never see Shooting Star again. Anger rose like bile when she became more and more convinced that someone had stolen her. She had no luck finding any water, and finally turned back. She'd only gone a hundred yards or so when she heard Chris calling her name.

As she rounded another bend she saw him, leading both horses, both of them saddled again.

"Geez, Miranda! I thought you'd been eaten by a bear or something. Were you planning to walk clear to the ocean in search of water?"

"No, but I, well, we gotta find water for the horses or go back. We can't keep pushing them in this heat without anything to drink."

"I know. Maybe we should go back and try to get some help. Maybe someone would bring us back in a jeep or something. There are hundreds of miles of little dips and hills and valleys where she could be, and we'd never see her."

"I know. And we don't even know if she's out here. If someone took her, she could be in Colorado or Canada by now."

"I'm sorry, Miranda. We just have to keep up hope. I know how much you love her. You're the one who's done all her training. I like her, too, but she's your horse more than anybody's."

Miranda felt the urge to cry. She bit her lip and turned her face away from Chris as she passed him. Her foot caught an exposed root, and she fell against him. He caught her in his arms, losing his balance and falling back on the edge of a gentle embankment. He didn't let go of Miranda, but cradled her gently in his arms. "Don't worry; we'll find her. We have to. I'll stick with you until we do. I promise."

Miranda buried her face in his shirt and sobbed. Chris wrapped strong arms around her and waited. When she finally lifted her face, he smiled at her, pulled the cotton bandana from around his neck and wiped her face with it.

She smiled back at him and sniffled. "Sorry," she said. "I..." But Chris's lips stopped her words. Miranda felt her body melt as his soft and tender mouth caressed hers. She kissed back, not wanting him to stop. Ever. But as his tongue sought hers and she thought her heart would explode, she pushed away and jumped to her feet.

"Christopher Bergman," she shouted. "Don't you ever do that again!" Seeing the look of shock on his reddening face and the sadness in his eyes, she softened her voice. "Promise me, please don't kiss me, okay?"

"I don't get you, Miranda." Chris's voice was angry, but Miranda knew him well enough to realize the anger was a cover up for badly hurt feelings. "You were kissing back, so don't try to tell me you hated it."

"I didn't hate it," Miranda said, pleading. "And that's the problem. Don't you see?

"No, I danged well don't see."

"Chris, you're my best friend. Well, next to Laurie, maybe. I like you. A lot. Too much."

"How can you like someone too much?" Chris continued to stare at her as he stood six feet away, his feet spread apart, and his hands on his hips. His face was dark and brooding.

He hardly has any freckles anymore, Miranda thought inanely. His sunburn had turned to tan and his red curls had bleached in the sun. He had become very good-looking, and she'd hardly noticed. She looked helplessly at him. "I don't know. I like you a lot. I'd do almost anything for you. I'd die for you. But I don't want to fall in love because I'm way too young, and it wouldn't last, and we'd get mad at each other, and we'd start hating each other, and I'd lose the best friend I ever had, and I'd be so sad. I..."

"Miranda, you're not making any sense. What the heck are you scared of? Do you think I'm going to hurt you? Do you think I'd take advantage of you and make you do something you don't want to do?"

"No, Chris. I don't think any of those things about you. It's me I'm scared of. I can't stand being so out of control of my feelings. And I truly am afraid of losing your friendship. I've seen it happen. Kids start going out and calling themselves a couple, and pretty soon something happens, and they get mad and don't ever speak to each other again. We're too young to be serious. We, we...we just can't fall in love, Chris. We have too much left to do first." Miranda faltered.

Chris emitted a short bitter laugh. "You make love sound like cancer or something. Well, have it your way. You always do. But you can't stop how I feel. Like it or not, I love you. I think I always have." Chris stomped past her, caught up Queen's reins, mounted, and headed back the way they'd come.

Miranda stood, staring at the retreating horse and rider. She slowly mounted Starlight and followed.

She shook her head ruefully. She remembered all the times she'd allowed herself to imagine a boy—some nondescript, handsome guy—saying "I love you. I think I always have." But never with an angry face—or in a tone of voice that sounded more like a scolding than a statement of love. *I'm so confused! Maybe by trying to keep our friendship the same, I've already lost it.*

Chapter Five

It was late afternoon when Chris and Miranda got back to the fairgrounds. They watered their horses, unsaddled them, and brushed them out—in silence. Although Miranda had caught up and ridden beside Chris all the way back, not a word had passed between them. When they returned to their campsite, Higgins was not there. Miranda grabbed a towel and changed into her swimming suit. Thankful to be camped next to the Little Big Horn River, she could hardly wait to cool off and rinse the sweat from her body. She had time for a quick dip before a second session of the Thursday powwow. Mary had told her that the grand entry for the evening session would begin at approximately 6 p.m.

When she got out of the water, Chris was gone. She quickly dressed and headed to the arbor, where the dances were held, arriving in time to watch the grand entry. She wished Chris had waited for her so they could sit together. She wanted to talk to him, but didn't know what she could say that would make things better between them. In a few minutes all her worries about her horse, her sadness for Laurie, and her mixed-up emotions about Christopher were washed away by the sights and sounds around her. Men, women, boys, and girls of all ages were dressed in fancy hand-beaded regalia. Numbers printed on white tags indicated those who would be competing for prizes in the dances that would follow the grand entry. She hoped she would have a number like that for the races tomorrow. If they'd let her, she'd still race Queen and Starlight.

Miranda stood with the rest of the crowd to greet the dancers led by the Veterans Honor Guard as they carried the Montana state flag, the United States Flag, and the Crow tribal flag. Hundreds of dancers took part in the grand entry. Miranda had hoped to be part of it. Mary Little Foot had even borrowed a beaded dress and moccasins for her to wear for the grand entry.

She wore it even though she still didn't have permission to participate. As she watched dance after dance, she was glad she wasn't a judge. All the participants danced well, as far as she could see. Her favorite dance competition was for girls about her age—until she saw the tiny tots. Kids no bigger than her five-year-old brother, Kort, were dressed in the finest beaded regalia and danced as well as older competitors.

"They are adorable. And look how well they dance," she exclaimed to anyone within hearing distance.

When she heard the announcer say, "Everybody dance!" Miranda wondered if that included her. She still hadn't been approved to participate. She watched as more people joined the circle, some in native traditional dress, some in jeans.

"Come, join us. It seems your spirit is already

united with the spirit of the dance," said a Crow woman she'd never met. The woman beckoned, and Miranda followed her to join the circle. The music with the beat of the drums seemed to carry her so that her feet barely touched the ground. Her spirit soared. She thought of nothing. She only felt the song inside her, joining her to those around her, making them one. Her worries and her weariness gone, nothing remained but the joy and excitement of the moment—a feeling that brought tears to her eyes and a smile to her face. She closed her eyes for a moment, and when she opened them, she saw Christopher's face. As he danced past her, he smiled, his blue eyes sparkled as they seemed to look deep into her soul—eyes full of happiness and friendship. She smiled back as he danced away, relieved to know that he was still her friend.

Miranda left the arbor before the dancing was over. She was tired and could hardly keep her eyes open. She wanted to get up early again to go searching for Star. As she was leaving she saw Mary Little Foot and went to say good night.

"Oh, I'm glad to see you," Mary said. "You've been approved to participate in the parade and grand entry and to compete in the races. I have your numbers for the competition. I'll get them to you in the morning before time for the parade. Which horse will you ride?"

"Really? Oh, wow. Good. Uh, I guess I'll ride Queen if I don't find Star in time. It's probably best not to take a stallion in a parade with lots of other horses."

"She's a beautiful horse. I'll help you dress her up

for the parade," Mary said, touching her lightly on the arm. "You'll make a lovely pair."

Miranda fairly bounced back to the tipi, but as she got ready for bed she sighed. She wished it could be Star. But there was still a chance that Star could show up, wasn't there? There were so many horses in the encampment that someone could have found her.

"Oh, I hope so." She whispered. Next to Starlight, she loved Shooting Star more than any horse. She was fast and flashy. She had a personality that Miranda admired. Independent and saucy, yet willing to let Miranda ride and guide her, as long as Miranda remembered that Shooting Star was in charge. She wanted her horse back, and the ache in that want was physical pain.

As she rode with Mary, the next morning, past those already lined up for the parade, Miranda was amazed at how many fine-looking horses there were. She had always thought her horses were more beautiful than any others, but, she had to admit, there were a lot of pretty horses and riders, enough to take her breath away.

After the parade, Miranda asked everyone she met if they had seen a loose filly the color of the darkest red of the sunset with a golden mane and tail. "She has a white star with a strip that goes down between her eyes, like a shooting star," Miranda said, "and white stockings, left front and right rear." No one had.

Soon it was time to line up for the race. The first was a sprint. She'd planned this one for Star, but since she was missing, Miranda entered Starlight. When Miranda joined the post parade, the procession in front of the grandstand, she was further impressed with the perfect conformation and beauty of the other contestants.

Emotions surged through her at the sight of them. Was it envy or jealousy—or maybe a little fear of the competition? She finally had to admit that she had not expected to see such excellence in horseflesh and skill in riders. They all seemed so natural and comfortable with horses. She'd watched tiny tots and kids of all ages ride in the parade and hold unofficial races with their ponies during the rodeo. They were every bit as good as she was.

I'm sure I'm not racist. I love the Indians, want to be one, so how could I have thought they'd have inferior horses and wouldn't know how to ride them as well as I can." She shook her head and reprimanded herself. *If I think like that, I don't deserve to be part of this.*

When it was time to get into the gate, Starlight went in easily. He'd been in gates like this before and seemed eager for what lay ahead. All the other horses went in, too, except for the one that was supposed to be in the gate next to Starlight's. She was proud of her horse, for he wasn't unnerved by the commotion of the horse fighting the handlers, rearing, backing up, and squealing.

The minute the horse went all the way in, the gates opened, and it kept running. Starlight lunged forward, but Miranda, who'd been watching the struggle, wasn't ready. To keep her balance, she jerked back on the reins, pulling Starlight slightly off balance as other horses surged past them. They were in last place! She corrected herself, stood in the stirrups, and leaned over his neck saying, "Go, boy, go!"

His muscles gathered under her and the power of his stride pulled them forward in a mighty thrust. Soon they were passing the pack, first one, then three, and finally there was only one horse in front of them—and there was the finish line. The other horse, a bay filly, was still ahead by a length.

Starlight finished second. That had never happened before. He had never lost a race. Miranda was stunned.

Queen's race at three in the afternoon was longer. Six furlongs. Miranda had learned her lesson. She made sure that she was ready and stayed ready, regardless of what was going on around her. Her eyes were straight ahead and her body tense, leaning forward, ready for action. Queen was eager and excited, bolting out of the gate the instant it opened and joining the front of the pack. Miranda gave her free rein, knowing her stamina was good for this race. As they neared the finish line, she noticed there were only two horses in front of her and Queen was passing them on the outside. Miranda leaned farther over her neck and shouted, "Go, girl. You can do it. You've got it. Go, go, go!"

And she did. Queen caught up to two horses who were fighting for the lead and joined them. In the end, a gray filly, also ridden by a girl, won by a neck, and it was too close to tell who was second. A beautiful bay gelding had tied with Queen.

After the race, Miranda waited to congratulate the girl who rode the gray.

"Thank you," the girl said. "Your horse is beautiful and very fast. You ride well." Miranda got the idea that she was thinking, but too kind to say, "for a white girl."

"Thanks. My name's Miranda Stevens. I know I don't look it, but I'm part Cherokee. That's why I got to enter, but I can see you could teach me a thing or two about riding."

A smile lit up the pretty girl's face. Miranda guessed her to be a year or two older than she was. "Thanks. My name is Naomi White-faced Horse. I'm Lakota and this is my second year to come to the Crow Fair to compete in the races. Storm Cloud won last year, too."

"Maybe we can get together later," Miranda said hopefully.

Naomi smiled and nodded. "Let's ride together in the parade in the morning," Naomi said.

Warmed by Naomi's friendliness, Miranda smiled as she rode Queen back to the campsite. Higgins and Chris met her there. They'd gone in the pickup to the grandstand to watch the race. It was too far from their camper for Higgins to walk. When she jumped off Queen, Chris held her reins. "What a horse, Queen. Now we can say you beat Starlight, can't we."

"No way," Miranda exclaimed taking Chris's bait. "How can you say that?"

"She came closer to winning her race and than he did. That's how." Chris's grin showed just how much he was enjoying this.

"Not fair. We should get to do that race over. The gate operator opened the gate before that horse ever stopped. It had a running start. And the rest of us weren't ready."

"Miranda are you blaming the gate operator for causing you to lose the race?" Higgins asked in an incredulous tone of voice.

"Yes. Didn't you see what happened?"

"I did indeed. They couldn't get the horse to go in and they opened the gate when they did."

"Yeah. That's what I mean. It's not fair."

"I didn't see the other riders have trouble getting started. The one who, as you say, had a running start isn't the one that beat you." Higgins was quiet for a moment and then asked, "If the shoe had been on the other foot, would you have cried foul?"

"Starlight would never have acted like that."

Higgins just looked at her and said nothing more. Miranda recalled something that she'd heard Mr. Taylor, Starlight's former owner, tell his jockey. He'd said, "Once your horse is in that gate, you may sit there several minutes while they get other horses set, but don't lose your focus. Stay tuned to your horse and the gate and nothing else. It can open when you least expect it."

She hadn't done that. Losing the race had been her fault. Starlight could have won without her. She only had to keep her balance, and she hadn't even done that.

Miranda rode Queen in the parade again the next morning. She was decked out in a colorful blanket that Mary Little Foot loaned her. Miranda let Mary braid her hair with a ribbon and some feathers in it. She rode next to Naomi and Cloud, admiring the Lakota girl's beauty and her horse's grace. Cloud held her head high and pranced along, seeming more joyful than nervous.

After the parade, she rode around the encampment asking everyone she met if they'd seen her horse. No one had. Most just shrugged, shook their heads, and moved on. She decided to go to the rodeo grounds. As she did so, she saw Shooting Star coming toward her, with a young man on her back in a western saddle.

Her heart leapt to her throat and she ran to meet them, but they turned off before she got close. "Hey, wait! You're on the horse. Wait. That's my horse."

The man looked in her direction and frowned. "Me?" he mouthed, pointing to himself.

By then Miranda was close enough to see that the horse he was riding was not her filly, but a gelding of the same color and the same white stocking on one back leg and a shorter sock on the front. As he turned his horse to face her, she saw that the strip on his face was longer than Star's and a little off center.

"Oh, I'm terribly sorry. From a distance your horse looked just like the one I lost yesterday morning. I'm frantic to find her and I thought..."

The rider shrugged and asked, "We okay, then?"

She nodded, her face burning with embarrassment.

Miranda changed her mind about going to the rodeo. She turned down the road to the encampment and put Queen in with Starlight. There was a race coming up after lunch. She'd better make sure Starlight was ready—that *she* was ready. She felt let down after thinking she'd found her horse, and she was still burning with embarrassment for accusing the young man.

She brushed Starlight's already glossy coat and told him her troubles. "One more race, Starlight. I'll do my best to keep my head in the right place and let you win this time. It's longer. You get to run all the way around the track. I know you'll like that."

Miranda was quiet for a while. "After that, no more races, so let's concentrate on finding Star. I still think she may be here. Someone may have caught her. We've just got to keep looking."

When post time drew near, Miranda put her lightweight English saddle on Starlight, slipped the bridle on him, and mounted up. She rode to the arena and race track, excited to have this chance to show people what he could really do.

The race went off without a hitch and Starlight won by two lengths without seeming to tire at all. "That's more like it. You're the best, Starlight."

"Wow, what a horse! Congratulations," Naomi White-faced Horse said, "I'm thinking of getting Cloud bred next summer. How much is your stud fee?"

Miranda didn't know the answer, but she exchanged contact information with Naomi, both girls promising to stay in touch.

At noon the next day, she went looking for Chris. She guessed he'd be at the concession stands near the arbor getting some food. On the way, she came upon a horse being led by a young woman. She was sure it was

Star, but didn't want to make a fool of herself again, so she trotted to catch up. "Excuse me, I just want to look at the horse you're leading."

The woman stopped. "She's a beauty, isn't she?" Indeed she was, but it didn't take long to see that she wasn't Star.

"Yes, she is," Miranda said, blinking back tears of disappointment. "I have—or had one that looks just like her, except mine has a star and a strip on her face instead of a full blaze. She got out of the corral when we first got here, and I've been looking for her ever since."

"Oh, I'm sorry to hear that. If I see a horse that could be yours, I'll let you know. Where are you staying?"

Miranda told her where their camper was parked by the river, next to Mary Little Foot's tipi.

Miranda turned back to the tipi, wiping at the tears running down her face. What would she do if she didn't find Shooting Star? Just one more day to search. She couldn't imagine going home without her.

Chapter Six

The Crow Fair came to an end all too soon. Ever since Star went missing Thursday morning, Miranda and Chris had looked for her every day. It was Monday, the parade was over, and Higgins—on Miranda's parents' orders—insisted they had to leave.

Before pulling onto I-90 to go home, Higgins directed Chris to pull into the gas station at Crow Agency to top off the tanks. Miranda fled to the restroom. Finding it empty she stared into the mirror. "I suppose you're going to cry now," she muttered to her reflection.

"Why shouldn't I?" she answered herself, resorting to a lifelong habit of carrying on a conversation with her reflection. "I insisted on bringing a horse here to show her off, and now she's gone. I didn't want to leave without finding her, but I have to. I'll probably never see her again." A tear trickled down her cheek.

Before the mirror-self could answer, she heard someone outside the door say, "Are you waiting for the rest room?" and another vice answered, "Yes."

She hurried to wash her hands and leave so someone else could come in. As she opened the door, a Crow woman stood in the narrow hallway and waited with a questioning look on her face."

"Just you?" she asked when no one else came out. "I thought I heard two people in there."

"Oh, uh, no. That was just me talking to myself." Miranda felt her face redden.

"I didn't mean to eavesdrop, but these walls are pretty thin. I can sympathize with your loss. I have also lost a loved one, only I still hold the hope that he will be found alive and returned to me."

"Oh, I'm sorry." Miranda was embarrassed to realize she'd been talking loudly enough for someone outside the door could hear what she said. "Who did you lose?"

"My grandson. He's only ten years old, but has seen way more than his share of sorrow. Now, I think he's in for a whole lot more."

"Why?"

The woman smiled at the young girl who was waiting, and told her to go ahead of her into the restroom. Then she answered, "I'm quite certain that his father kidnapped him."

"Won't he be okay with his dad?"

"Only if his father doesn't drink. And that's like saying if only eagles don't fly. Even when he's not drinking, he's a bad influence. We are an honest people, but once in a while someone like my son-in-law spoils our reputation. I don't want my grandson learning how to steal."

"I sure hope they find him. I wish I could help," Miranda said, meaning it.

"How did your horse die?" the woman asked.

"Oh, she didn't die. She's lost. She somehow got

out of the corral, something she's good at. But I looked for her all weekend, so I think maybe she was stolen. Chances of getting a stolen horse back are slim to none, or so my friend, Higgins, told me. He should know. He's been taking care of horses his whole life—and he's old—but the hardest thing is giving up looking for her. I tried looking for her around here, just in case she had just run away, but the country's too big. I just don't think she'd go that far on her own and not come back to the other horses, so it really looks like she was stolen. She's probably in another state by now." Miranda couldn't seem to slow down or stop talking once she started. It seemed she had to either pour her heart out or cry.

"Then you can still have hope, as I do. Until your horse—and my grandson—are found, we need to believe they will be returned to us."

"Thanks, but that's kind of hard to do."

"It's the only way. Follow your heart and believe that what you want will come to you."

"Thanks. I'll be thinking of your grandson, too. I hope he comes back to you soon."

"Here's his picture. I'm giving it to everyone I see in the hope that someone will see him and call me. You might want to do the same with your horse's picture if you have one."

"Okay. How can I get hold of you?"

The woman handed her a business card. *Lucille Spotted Owl, Artist.* The card had the address of an art gallery, a phone number, and an email address. Then she handed Miranda a clipping from the *Billing's*

Gazette. It was an article about the boy's disappearance, suggesting that his father had kidnapped him. A boy's picture and that of a man filled the bottom half of the first page. "His name is Teddy. Teddy Hungry Horse."

"Thanks. I'd better go now. I'll read this in the truck. And I'll send you a picture of my horse." Miranda felt a bond with this grandmother. She seemed so full of love and sadness, yet she spoke of hope. Maybe they could help each other.

"Send me several copies. I'll show them around. Someone might have seen her." She put a hand on Miranda's arm. "And here's something to think about. Like I said, we are an honest people, and it's hard to imagine anyone at the fair stealing a horse, but I wouldn't put it past my former son-in-law."

Before Miranda could get her wits together to say more, the girl came out of the restroom and Lucille went in and closed the door.

"It's about time," Chris growled, when she climbed into the back seat. He started the truck and pulled away from the pumps, watching the trailer in his rear-view mirror.

"If I had my way, I'd stay until I found Star," Miranda growled as she buckled her seatbelt and settled back to look at the clipping. "I met someone, and we got to talking."

"A good-looking Indian boy, probably," Chris said, sounding jealous.

"Um, yeah," Miranda teased, spreading the paper out on her lap. "Very good-looking, I'd say."

When Chris didn't answer, she looked at his face in the mirror. He stared straight ahead, his mouth pinched in a thin line.

"But actually, it was the cute guy's grandma that I talked to. Her grandson has been kidnapped. His dad just escaped from jail. I guess he isn't supposed to see his son at all, and now, apparently, he has him and is hiding him somewhere," Miranda said as she read the paper and the captions under the pictures. "And she thinks it's possible that he stole our horse when he kidnapped his son."

Chris raised his eyebrows. "Whoa! That's the best lead we've had. We'd better do whatever we can to help find him."

"I saw the news of a jail break in the paper a few days ago." Higgins turned to look at her. "I wonder if it's the same guy?"

Miranda held up the picture of the escapee.

"Yep. Same one. Donald Hungry Horse. He was in the Big Horn County Jail awaiting trial for embezzlement."

"Oh, so that's what the grandmother meant about not wanting the boy to learn to steal." She looked more closely at the image of the boy, probably a school picture. He was grinning widely, and his dark hair had a rumpled look as the front of it stood straight up. A braid on each side hung over his shoulders. "I don't know how he feels about his father, but I know his grandma was worried that he wouldn't be safe if the father started drinking. I hope they catch him soon. The boy's only ten years old."

"What's his grandmother like?" Chris asked.

"She's very nice. Pretty. But she sure looked sad and worried. I have her address so I can keep in touch. I really like her."

Unloading just two horses back at Heavenly Acres Horse Ranch was sadder than she could have imagined. Long after Chris left to take Higgins home, Miranda brushed Starlight. She didn't even talk to him as usual, because her voice was too full of tears. Starlight seemed to understand. When she finally put the brush down and wrapped her arms around his neck, he turned his head pressing it against her back in a hug. Miranda let out a big sigh. "I love you more than anything, Starlight. At least I have you, and maybe we'll get your daughter back. We've got to." Tears dampened Starlight's neck.

Mom and Dad both gave her a comforting hug when she came back in the house. That made it even harder to keep from crying. She was thankful that Mom didn't say, "I-told-you-so," just "I'm so sorry Miranda. Maybe we'll find her."

The phone rang early the next morning just as the family finished breakfast. Margot raced to answer it as if she were expecting a phone call. She looked disappointed when she handed Miranda the phone.

"Hello?"

"Miranda, it's me, Laurie. We just got home last night. I want to hear all about the Crow Fair."

"I have so much to tell you. Can you come over?"

"Yes, Mom said she'd bring me. I can't wait to see Lady. Did you race her at the fair?"

"No. I wouldn't do that without your permission. I raced Queen and Starlight. But I couldn't race Star. I lost her." Miranda's voice broke and she couldn't go on.

"What? Really? What do you mean?"

"I'll tell you when you get here," Miranda managed to say.

"I'll be there in ten minutes." The phone clicked off.

Miranda hurried to clear the table, telling her mom that she and Laurie were going riding and would need a lunch.

"There are sandwich fixings and all kinds of fruit in the refrigerator," Mom said, "and three kinds of cookies in the cookie jar. Margot baked a fresh batch of peanut butter cookies yesterday."

"Thanks, Mar," Miranda said, blowing her little sister a kiss.

"Can I go, too?" five-year-old Kort asked.

"Too? Too?" echoed one-year-old Kaden as he toddled across the floor on chubby legs, holding his arms out for balance.

"Not this time, sweeties, maybe later."

Laurie and Miranda rode side by side through the pasture, talking about everything that had happened to each of them while they were apart. Miranda told about losing Star, the horror she felt when she noticed she was missing, and how hope of finding her drained away as time went by.

"Something happened when we were out looking for her," Miranda said as they sat in a sunny clearing, finishing their sandwiches. "Chris and I went looking for Star right away. When we stopped to eat…" Miranda haltingly told Laurie about walking up the draw, meeting and falling into Chris's arms. "And then we kissed."

"What's wrong with that?" Laurie asked.

"Everything. Don't you see? It's just infatuation, but it makes me feel like I can't live without him."

"So, what is wrong with that?" Laurie asked again. "Call it whatever you want, but it's love, and love is good."

"Is that what you have with Bill?"

"Yes. Whether it's infatuation or puppy love—as the grownups like to call it—I know what I feel—and it's love. Bill loves me and I love him, and we are good to each other and good for each other, and I don't see anything wrong with that."

Miranda remained doubtful. "I'm just so mixed up. I would die if I lost Chris as a friend. I just don't want him to think he owns me."

"Miranda, you aren't making sense. I don't know what you're so afraid of. Do you think he'd try to own you?"

Miranda shrugged. They were both silent for a while, lost in their own thoughts.

"Oh, I almost forgot," Laurie exclaimed, breaking the silence. "It might not be important, and I didn't want to worry you, but you should know—just in case."

"What?"

"I heard something on the radio when we were driving home. I didn't catch the whole name, but it got me to thinking about the guy that tried to kill you and Starlight. I think they said, 'Hicks.' Wasn't that the guy's name? Where was he from?"

"Yeah. Martin Hicks. He'd escaped from a mental institution—somewhere in Ohio. What about him?"

"Well, if it's the same one, he escaped again. There's a manhunt out for him, and they think he's dangerous."

Hicks! She suddenly felt numb as she remembered the madman who'd worked for Mr. Taylor. He'd been afraid of Starlight and went after him with a pitchfork. Miranda tried to protect her horse and Hicks swore he'd get even with her. When Mr. Taylor fired him, he blamed both Miranda and Starlight and came back for revenge. Together, Miranda and Starlight fought the man for their lives. Hicks had been arrested and returned to Ohio.

When Miranda found her voice, she said, "If it's him, he will probably come after me. He's just crazy enough that he won't forget until he gets his revenge."

Chapter Seven

Every day, as Miranda did her chores, she found herself looking for Shooting Star among the herd. The realization that she wasn't there and probably never would be hit her like a punch in the stomach, and the sadness welled up inside her all over again. It wasn't getting any better. She wanted her horse back, and no one was doing a thing about it. She wasn't doing a thing about it, and that depressed her most of all. But what could she do that she hadn't already done?

Her mind flew in every direction as she wondered what could have happened to her beautiful Shooting Star. Had Martin Hicks taken her? Killed her? How would he know where she was? That Star was her horse? She finally let go of that idea when she learned that Hicks hadn't escaped until the day after Star disappeared.

What about Teddy Hungry Horse's father? He was still at large. Lucille would have called her if they'd found him. Miranda remembered her words. "I wouldn't put anything past Donald Hungry Horse."

Miranda didn't want to accept that she'd never see her horse again, but the more time passed, the more depressed she became. She just hoped whoever had her was being good to her.

After three months with no word about Shooting Star, Miranda plodded through her classes, doodling in the margins of her notebook as teachers droned on about lessons. Her test scores dropped, and her teachers complained.

"Miranda, please see me after class," her algebra teacher, Mrs. Englemaier, said just before the bell rang.

Miranda sank back into her desk and folded her arms, waiting. When the classroom cleared, the teacher asked, "What's going on with you, Miranda? I know you can do this work. You got A's and B's in eighth grade math. This isn't that much different."

Miranda shrugged.

"Is something wrong at home?" Mrs. E. asked. "Are your parents fighting or sick or anything like that?"

"No! We're great. Everyone is fine."

"Well, Miranda. You don't seem fine. Something is bothering you. Is it boyfriend trouble?"

"I don't have a boyfriend, which is fine with me." Miranda thought of Chris—and the kiss—and she felt like her stomach flipped, but she went on. "And my friends and I are getting along fine."

It was true that Chris had given up the foolishness about being in love with her and hadn't said a word about it since they got back from the fair. With Laurie back, they were once again the do-everything-together threesome, sometimes joined by Bill. They just did it more quietly as they grieved their losses separately.

"Then why don't you tell me what it is, Miranda? You haven't got mixed up with drugs, have you?

"No! I'm not stupid!"

Mrs. E. raised one eyebrow and held Miranda's gaze.

"Okay. I lost a horse, and I can't help thinking about her. I have no way of knowing where she is or whether I'll ever get her back. Everyday that I don't hear anything makes me that much more sure that I never will."

"I'm so sorry to hear that. I'm sure that must worry you." Mrs. E. paused a moment before going on hesitantly. "I've heard that you have several horses. Is that true?"

"Yes. Why?"

"Well, maybe if you could concentrate on being grateful for the ones you still have, you could move past the disappointment and get back to working on the responsibilities of the present."

Stunned, Miranda stared at the teacher. Finally, she leaned forward and asked in a quiet, controlled voice, "How many children do you have, Mrs. Englemaier?"

"I have four."

"So, if one of them disappeared without a trace, you'd just say, 'I'm so grateful that I still have three that I won't worry about this lost one.' Is that right?"

Miranda stood, glared at the teacher who looked as if she'd just been slapped. "I didn't think so," Miranda said and left the room.

When Miranda got home, she was still shaking with anger. She went straight to the barn, grabbed Starlight's bridle, and headed for the pasture.

"Where are you going, Mandy? Aren't you waiting for Chris and Laurie?"

Miranda stopped and waited for Margot to catch up. "If they come tell them I'll be back, but they should ride without me. And tell Mom, too. Tell her I'm fine. I just need to exercise Starlight."

"She's gonna be mad."

"No she won't. Tell her I'll explain everything when I get back. I just need to be alone for a while, Margot."

When Miranda approached her black stallion, he lifted his head from grazing and walked toward her. When they met, he lowered his head. She put her palm against his forehead, and he pressed into it. She wrapped her arms around him, cradling his elegant head in her arms.

"You understand, don't you, boy? You probably miss her, too. She's your little girl, you know." Miranda let her tears flow freely now that no one but her horse would see them. "What if we don't ever find her?" She sobbed softly and pulled away. "Let's run through the river pasture and up to the top of Silver Butte. I think we'll both feel better with some wind in our faces."

She slipped the bridle over his nose and eased the bit into his mouth. He lowered his head, making it easy to slide the headstall over his ears and fasten the throatlatch.

"Now, to get on you. I'm not fooling with a saddle today." She led him through a gate and into a nearly dry stream bed where he could stand while she jumped on from the bank. Miranda was tall for her age, but at 16 and 3/4 hands Starlight was still hard to mount without a saddle. He'd learned to stand patiently until she was seated, unlike the first time she'd tried to ride him when he was not yet two years old and untrained.

Miranda urged Starlight into an easy lope all the way to the river and the well-worn path beside it. Slowing to an easy walk, Miranda took in the beauty of the clear water as it tumbled over rocks of all colors. The view was mostly unobstructed as only a few leaves clung to the uppermost boughs of the cottonwood trees.

Miranda had ridden Shooting Star along this very trail just two days before the Crow Fair. She'd behaved very well until a flock of pinion jays lifted as one great blanket from the ground in front of her. The filly had bolted sideways, almost unseating Miranda, and then ran full out down the trail. Miranda hadn't tried to stop her, but had leaned over her neck and urged her on, thrilled to feel how incredibly fast she was. Miranda had wished she could find someone willing to ride her in a race with Starlight. She'd love to know which one would win. Could she possibly be faster than her sire? *I'll probably never find out*, she thought.

She leaned forward. "Let's go, Starlight. Like the wind."

With no more urging than that, Starlight bolted to a full run and thundered down the path and up the hill, not stopping until they came to the flat top of Silver Butte.

"Way to go, boy. You're the best. I'll always miss Shooting Star, but thank God I didn't lose you."

Margot had been right. Mom was foot-stomping mad

when Miranda returned an hour late for supper.

"Don't you ever take off like that again without asking me! I was worried sick. And two little boys who'd waited all day to see you cried their eyes out when you didn't come home."

"Really? Kortie and Kaden cried?"

"Kort cried because you didn't come home. He is expecting you to keep your promise to take him riding. Kaden cried because Kort was bawling."

All of the excuses and arguments that Miranda had rehearsed evaporated as remorse took their place. She adored her little brothers.

"Where are they?" Miranda started toward the nursery.

"They're asleep, of course, though it wasn't easy calming them down. Don't you wake them!"

Miranda turned back. "I'm sorry, Mom."

"Whatever possessed you to be so irresponsible?"

"Mom, I just had to get off by myself before I exploded," Miranda said, recalling all the excuses she'd prepared. "Mrs. Englemaier made me so mad, I was ready to kill someone."

"Watch it, Miranda. Don't say things you don't mean. You know you were not ready to kill anyone," said a voice behind her.

"Dad! How long have you been standing there?" Miranda, who'd do anything to please her father, spun toward the kitchen door at the sound of his voice.

"Long enough to hear your poor excuse. I don't care how upset you are with a teacher or anyone else, you don't treat your family like that. We were all worried. Mar had to do your chores, and your mother was so worried that the boys were sure that something terrible had happened to you. We couldn't tell them differently, because we didn't know."

"I'm sorry. I just didn't think."

"That's always been your problem, Miranda. You don't think things through," Mom said. "I thought you'd gotten better, but this is the worst. What took you so long? Did you get thrown?"

"No," Miranda said, hanging her head. "When we got to the top of Silver Butte, Starlight just seemed like he wanted to keep going, so we just kept walking. I didn't realize how late it was until the sun started to set."

"That's lame, Miranda. You're going to blame your horse? Did you ever once think about how your mother would worry? About your chores or your friends or your homework?" Dad asked.

"Did Laurie and Chris come?"

"Yes, and waited until almost dark for you. Now answer my question."

"No. I guess I didn't think about anyone but myself. I thought everyone would understand."

"You are the one who needs to understand. That kind of irresponsibility will not be tolerated. I know you're worried about Shooting Star, but worry won't bring her back." Dad's face was stern and Miranda had to look away. She knew she deserved whatever he would mete out.

"You're grounded, Miranda. From riding."

Miranda jerked her head up to look in his eyes. He couldn't be serious. His face told her he was.

"For how long?"

"Until your grades come back up to a B average. And until you've proven that you can take responsibility for your share of the work around here. You will come straight home from school and do your chores and—Margot's, too, for the next two days. You will play with the boys, and study. If you've brought your grades up by the end of the semester, you can go back to riding."

"But Dad! That's not until after Christmas."

"I know. By then you will realize the seriousness of putting your self pity ahead of everyone else."

"Now, why were you so angry at your teacher?" Mom asked.

Miranda repeated the conversation including her own clever remarks that had left the teacher speechless.

"You apologize to her tomorrow," Mom said.

"What? Me apologize to her?"

"Indeed," her father said. "She was trying to help, and your thanks was to cut her down with hurtful words?"

"You've got to grow up, Miranda. Life doesn't stop because you're sad or worried, no matter how great your loss. You still have a responsibility, not only to others, but to yourself." Mom stood, squeezed Miranda's arm, and looked straight into her eyes. "So get over it and get on with your life."

Miranda gaped at Mom's retreating back.

Mom turned. "Come talk to this one. He's still awake.

He's been crying because he was afraid you were dead. I told him you surely weren't, but I couldn't prove it, could I?"

Miranda gasped and ran to enfold Elliot in her arms. How could she have so thoughtlessly hurt this child who had already seen his mother and then his beloved grandfather die. He was only ten years old, but far wiser and stronger, Miranda thought, than she was.

"Oh, Elliot! I'm so sorry I scared you like that. So, so sorry." Elliot dissolved into sobs of relief. Miranda's tears dampened his tousled hair. She'd fallen in love with this sweet child when he'd first come to live with Mr. Taylor at Shady Hills Ranch when he was six. When her parents were given custody of Elliot after Mr. Taylor died less than a year ago, Miranda had welcomed him into their home with joy to have him as a little brother. Seeing how she'd cracked his tenuous hold on his emotions, she knew she didn't deserve the devotion he gave her. But she determined to do all she could to do better—and never again trigger his fear of losing yet another loved one.

Chapter Eight

Miranda didn't wait until sixth period when she'd be in Mrs. Englemaier's class. She needed to get the apology over with and start the day fresh. She hated having to admit she was wrong, but it seemed to be a steady diet for her. She'd apologized to Margot, Kort, and even baby Kaden when they got up that morning. She couldn't have been more remorseful than she was when she saw Kort looking around the kitchen with big, teary eyes before he spotted her and ran to throw his arms around her neck.

"I'm so sorry I scared you," she'd said, for what seemed like the dozenth time. "I'm okay, really. I wasn't thinking how you'd feel. I'm so sorry." And she meant it. How could she have forgotten these little guys who looked up to her and trusted her?

She'd felt less remorse when she apologized to Margot who just seemed angry rather than hurt or scared. "Sorry you had to do my chores, Margot, but don't feel bad. I have to do yours double."

Miranda was never sure what Margot thought or how she felt. She had a way of keeping it all to herself—unlike Miranda. This difference in them often made their relationship difficult. Margot, like Elliot, had been through a lot of heartbreak, having lost her mother in a boating accident and then farmed out to strangers by a father who obviously didn't want her. She'd come to live with Miranda and her grandparents. That was before Miranda's father had come back from the dead and while her mother was still in California.

Dad hadn't really been dead, of course, but for years Miranda hadn't known whether he was dead or alive. He'd left before Miranda was born. When she finally heard that he had enlisted in the Navy and that he was swept off the deck of an aircraft carrier into the middle of a very stormy Atlantic Ocean, she, like everyone else, assumed he was dead. What a miracle it had seemed when he returned. The best part was to learn that he loved her and hadn't been willingly absent from her life.

Miranda thought she'd been through a lot, but she conceded that losing a loving mother as Margot had, must be much harder than never knowing your father until he suddenly showed up, just when she needed him most. Miranda silently vowed to be more understanding of her quiet sister, but it wasn't always easy.

Miranda brushed thoughts of Margot from her mind when she got to the classroom where Mrs. Englemaier sat at her desk shuffling papers. Miranda cleared her throat, and the teacher looked up.

"Miranda, come in. What can I do for you this morning?" Mrs. E's smile was bright, though she wore a puzzled look.

Miranda rushed in and leaned across the desk. "Mrs. E., I came to apologize."

"What for, Miranda?"

"For being rude yesterday, for one. What I said was so disrespectful. You were trying to help me, and I was just feeling sorry for myself."

"Any word on your horse?"

Miranda shook her head. "No. Nothing's changed except for me seeing how self-centered I've been. I still desperately want to find Shooting Star, but moping and forgetting that other people besides me exist won't bring her back. In fact, if Grandma is right, it'll be the opposite. Negative thinking brings negative results, according to her. And I believe it. Still, it's hard to believe I'll find Star after such a long time."

"Well, I accept your apology, Miranda. Thank you."

"Uh, thanks, but I have one more thing to apologize for. Neglecting my homework and not paying attention in class." Mrs. E raised her eyebrows, and Miranda hurried on. "Grandpa reminded me that I have a responsibility to do my best in school. It's a privilege to get a free education, and I don't have the right to blow it off like it's nothing."

"You have very wise grandparents. I'm glad you're listening to them."

"Yeah. They're pretty smart." Miranda grinned, but didn't explain that she'd been sent to their house to apologize to them before she could have any supper. It was only fair. They worried about Miranda as much as anyone did.

Miranda experienced her emotions very strongly. Convinced of her mistake, she wholeheartedly threw herself into making up for the selfish pining and sulking she'd engaged in since Shooting Star disappeared.

A week later, when Miranda stepped off the bus a snowball slammed into the side of her face. She dropped her backpack to scoop up snow as she looked for her assailant. She formed a ball and threw it at Chris as he ran across the lawn toward her.

"Bull's-eye!" she yelled as her snowball knocked his cap off.

"I surrender," Chris yelled. "Cease fire! I have something to show you."

Miranda picked up her backpack and took the newspaper Chris held out to her.

The headline he pointed to read, "Donald Hungry Horse Captured," and the article began, "After being arrested Friday morning at a tavern in Minot, North Dakota, Donald Hungry Horse, who escaped from jail months ago, will now face additional charges." Miranda scanned the brief article. Mr. Hungry Horse had been involved in an altercation and had pulled a knife on a man before the tavern owner called 911 and then subdued him. She read to the end where it said he was returned to custody.

"But it doesn't say anything about his son—or our horse," Miranda said, "Maybe we were wrong about that."

"He probably sold Shooting Star, somehow," Chris said. "He'd need money."

"But what about his kid, Teddy? Do you suppose the little boy is locked up in a room somewhere, and the police don't even know about him?"

"Wouldn't his grandma have told them about the boy?" Chris said. "After all, that first article she showed you said they suspected that he'd kidnapped his son."

"I have to call her and find out what she knows."

"At least it gives us a lead for where to look for our horse," Chris said. "We thought he'd probably taken her to Wyoming or Idaho. Maybe he sold her somewhere in eastern Montana or North Dakota."

"Yeah, I guess it's something. But if it's true, whoever bought her isn't going to answer our ads."

"What ads?" Chris asked.

"The ones we'll put in the papers in that part of the state and in North Dakota. Maybe South Dakota, too. Who knows where he might have been all this time."

"What's the point if whoever bought her won't answer anyway?"

"Maybe someone who has seen the horse and knows who the buyer is will call us."

"Why don't we go to the jail and talk to him? Or get the sheriff to question him?" Chris suggested.

"Yeah. Like he's going to confess to kidnapping and stealing a horse, even if he did." Miranda folded the paper. "Thanks for bringing this. I'm going to call Mom."

Mom said, No, Miranda absolutely could not skip school. And, no, she wasn't going to look for the number to call the boy's grandmother. "You need to concentrate on school and let law enforcement do their job."

The day crept by. When Miranda finally got home, she went to her room to get the phone number for Lucille Spotted Owl.

"Margot, have you been messing with my stuff? I had a business card right here on my chest of drawers."

"No. I dusted, but I put everything back like it was."

"I've told you not to clean my room.

"It's my room, too. And I like it neat."

"Help me pull this out so I can look behind it."

"Miranda, phone!" Mom called from the kitchen.

"Okay, just a minute."

"Now," Mom said, appearing in the door of the girls' bedroom and holding out the phone.

Miranda sighed, grabbed the phone, and said, "Hello," in a less than friendly tone.

"Miranda, this is Lucille Spotted Owl."

"Oh! Good! I was just looking for your number so I could call you. They caught the guy that kidnapped your grandson, but the newspaper didn't say anything about him. Do they know? Has anyone found the boy?"

"That's why I'm calling you. Apparently, he didn't take the boy. He swears he doesn't know anything about him. The sheriff is also convinced he didn't take him."

"But he'd lie, wouldn't he? He'd never admit that he did it or that he stole a horse."

"I've talked to him myself. He's a liar, all right. Always has been, but I can tell when he's telling the truth. This is one of those times."

"Then where is your grandson? Where is my horse? Did someone else take them? I guess the two disappearing at the same time was a coincidence and have nothing to do with each other. Is that what you think?"

"No, it isn't. I think they have everything to do with each other. Here is why..." Lucille drew a deep breath, sounding as if she were having difficulty going on. "A friend of mine went hunting near the Pryor Mountains on the first day of hunting season and found an old campfire and a deer carcass. Some meat had been cut off of it. A mountain lion was at it when he arrived. Someone had shot it with an arrow."

"What does that have to do with your grandson? It would take a grown man to kill a deer with a bow and arrow. Do you think someone's with him?"

"Teddy got a hunting bow for Christmas last year. It's small enough for him to handle, but it's not a toy. I looked for it today, and it's not in his room. Then I noticed that my sleeping bag is missing from the closet where I always keep it, and I found that some camping supplies are also missing along with my backpack. It's larger than Teddy's, which is still in his room."

"So you think he ran away and is hiding out, camping somewhere in the mountains?" Miranda didn't see how a ten-year-old could even get there, let alone survive all that time. The Pryor Mountains weren't close, or she and Chris might have searched in that direction.

"Yes. That's what I think, and I wouldn't be surprised to find out he's riding your horse."

"But, she's pretty hard to handle. And I still have her halter and bridle. Did he take yours?"

"No. I don't know where he might have gotten one—if he did, but I still suspect that he might have your horse."

"It's been so long. How could a kid that young possibly survive?"

"You don't know Teddy," Lucille said, as if that answered everything. "Are you willing to come join the hunt."

"Yes! I'll have to ask my parents of course, but I'm sure Dad will let me. I'll bring my horse, Shooting Star's father. If she's out there, and we get close, he'll find her."

"Hurry. The forecast is for a severe snowstorm by the end of the week. I'll meet you near the Pryor mountains at eight tomorrow morning."

"How will we find you?"

"Drive east out of the town of Pryor until you see my pickup and horse trailer parked in a driveway. I have a friend who has a ranch we can drive through to get to the mountains."

Chapter Nine

Miranda scanned the sky as she got out of the ranch truck to meet Lucille Spotted Owl. Dark clouds rose above the western horizon. Otherwise, the sky was deep blue and cloudless. The sun was still low in the morning sky. She and Dad had left home a little after four a.m. They pulled in behind Lucille's rig at fifteen minutes after eight.

Lucille walked back to meet Miranda. "Leave your horses in the trailer and follow me. We can drive most of the way before we need to travel on horseback," Lucille told her as she hurried to the driver's side of the ranch truck where Dad was just getting out. "Hi, I'm Lucille Spotted Owl. Thank you for coming and bringing Miranda."

"I'm Barry Stevens, Miranda's father," he said, shaking her proffered hand.

Lucille nodded and stepped back. "I'll lead the way."

The gravel road that Lucille led them on wound through meadows, over hills, and through gullies. It became rougher and more narrow, the farther they went.

Lucille finally parked on a grassy hill overlooking a deep ravine that separated them from the steep side of a tree-covered mountain.

Miranda hurried to unload Starlight. They had brought the four-horse trailer rather than the smaller one, in the hope that they'd be taking three horses home, not just two. As Miranda tightened the saddle on Starlight, Lucille unloaded a bay gelding, already saddled, with saddlebags and a rain slicker secured behind the cantle. Lucille put a bridle over his halter and mounted. Dad readied and mounted Queen. Chris, who'd begged his parents, to no avail, to let him skip school to go with Miranda, readily agreed to let Dad borrow his mare for the search.

"This is familiar country to my family. We often hunt in this area. We'll ride together through the ravine and then I'll go one way and you two the other. I don't know which direction Teddy would take. He loved it all.

Miranda looked at the looming thunderhead and said to Lucille. "I thought the weather was supposed to be nice until the weekend. I hope those clouds go the other way."

"I hope so, too. We'd better get started, though, in case they don't."

As they rode toward the mountain, Miranda said, "I'm sorry we didn't get here sooner. I hope you didn't have to wait long. You must be worried about Teddy."

"Worry is a substitute for action, so I don't worry. I spent last night and the early morning getting ready, both physically and spiritually." She turned to smile at Miranda. "We are going to find him."

"But it's been three months! How could he get along out here?" Miranda stared at the ruggedness of the mountain. No white boy or girl that Miranda knew or had ever heard of would attempt such a feat, let alone survive it. She remembered the winter night she'd run away with Starlight. The two nights she spent in a cave seemed long. It wouldn't have been possible for her to live away from civilization for three months.

"Teddy is Apsáalooke through and through—a proud Crow who has been begging me to let him go on a vision quest for more than a year now. His hero is the late Chief Plenty Coups who went on his first vision quest when he was only nine." Lucille shook her head ruefully. "Teddy liked to remind me of that, but I kept putting him off, thinking as you do, that he is too young. Who am I to judge that? We will see."

Lucille stopped her horse. "Here is where we go our separate ways. I'll go left and explore that drainage over there. You two take this one. There is a small stream in it that he may have tried to follow. If we spread out, we have a better chance of finding him before dark."

"Let's meet back at the trailers by five-thirty" Dad said. "That's less than eight hours from now."

Lucille agreed and they parted ways.

They set off in a ground-eating trot, but before the hill got very steep, Dad cursed and stopped. "Hold up, Miranda. Something's wrong with Queen."

Miranda turned back as her Dad dismounted and ran his hand down Queen's right foreleg.

"What's wrong?"

"She started limping pretty badly," Dad said, "Oh here it is. She ran a stick into her leg. It's pretty deep."

He pulled the stick, a jagged piece of hawthorn, from her pastern and blood poured down her leg. "I'd better take her back to the trailer and doctor it. We have ointment and bandages and wrap in the pickup. You'd better come with me. She might not be fit for mountain climbing even after I wrap it.

"But Dad, why should I come back? I can be looking for Teddy."

"I don't like you going up there alone."

"Why? I can't possibly get lost. I'll follow the stream up and back down again. And I can see the trailers from here."

"Yes, but what if you get hurt up there by yourself?"

"I won't. If I do, I'll ride back down. We've got to find Teddy and Shooting Star before the weather gets bad. You let me ride in the hills and pasture alone at home."

"Well, okay, but be sure you're back to the trailers before dark. Turn around at noon or twelve-thirty whether you've found them or not."

"But Dad, it's always faster coming down hill. What if I'm this close to finding them when I have to turn around?"

"No, it's not always faster coming down. Sometimes it takes longer. Turn around at noon. Promise me, Miranda."

"Twelve thirty," Miranda said. "Or at least before one."

"Miranda, promise!"

"Okay. I won't be late," Miranda muttered as she turned Starlight toward the mountain.

Dad walked back into the trees in the ravine, leading Queen. Miranda turned up the trail to the mountain. Alone, she let Starlight ease into his trot over dry grass and sagebrush until the mountain became too steep. The summer had been hot and dry, but late September had brought cooler temperatures with rain and snow. Then the weather had turned warm for more than a month with lows hovering around the freezing mark and highs in the 60s and 70s, rare for November in Montana.

Starlight jogged on, alert, but not alarmed, and all seemed well and right with the world. Miranda couldn't stop looking around. She loved the look, smell, and feel of the hills. The air was so fresh her nose tingled and she drew in deep gulps of it to the bottom of her lungs. She saw the occasional flash of a whitetail deer's tail as it waved a retreating warning. She heard the gentle ripple of the small stream she followed. An occasional croak of a raven and the eerie cry of the red-tailed hawk thrilled her. This was her element. Every time she came rode in any mountains, she felt that she was home.

As Miranda let Starlight pick his way around trees, boulders, and rock outcroppings, she scanned the landscape for signs that another horse had been there. A rabbit sprang from beneath Starlight's feet. He paid little attention to it. Miranda remembered Star's reaction to a bounding bunny.

"Good boy," Miranda said. "If that had been Shooting Star, she would have jumped sideways and dumped her rider in a pile of cactus or a rock. Then she'd have run away—and good luck catching her!" Miranda sighed as she imagined the scene. "I sure hope we find that kid alive. If he stole Star, he has a lot of explaining to do!"

As the trail grew steeper, Starlight lunged forward. His long legs pulled them upward without much effort.

They had to slow down when the ravine narrowed and timber thickened. Clouds now covered the sun, adding a chill to the air.

"I feel like we're looking for a needle in a haystack. If Teddy and Star are in these hills, and that's a stretch if you ask me, they could just as well be at the other end of the mountain range," Miranda complained to her horse as he picked his way through the dry underbrush, weaving between trees.

Starlight stopped, bringing Miranda's attention back to the path—or lack thereof—ahead of them. The rocks ahead were too steep to climb. "I don't see any way to go up without going down first," There seemed no way around the thick jumble of junipers and dry downfall between them and the stream. She dismounted and led Starlight back a few steps and then away from the stream around a tree and some boulders and up a steep side hill. She walked off to the side of the narrow path to allow Starlight to scramble up beside and ahead of her. She dropped his reins as he passed her so he could keep climbing until he came to a level spot where he waited for her.

She shivered and looked up at thickening clouds. She could no longer see any blue sky.

She zipped up her coat and remounted. "We're getting too far from the stream, don't you think? Let's angle in that direction and keep climbing. As soon as we find water, we'll stop for lunch." It had been hours since she'd eaten, and she figured Starlight would be thirsty, for even though it was far from hot out, he was beginning to sweat from the exertion.

A little higher up, the hill became a gentle upward slope and they picked up another deer trail that led toward the creek. As the sound of running water became audible and grew louder, the trail widened. Miranda pulled Starlight to a stop when she saw the series of small waterfalls cascading above her. Where the stream crossed the trail, it became a broad, shallow pool before it tumbled down a steep slope to disappear over a rocky ledge.

"Perfect place to eat our lunch, Starlight," Miranda said, dismounting. "I'll loosen your cinch so you can relax while I sit on that rock up there and eat my sandwich." Miranda removed the bridle and put his halter on, letting the lead rope drag. "Drink up, boy."

The air was still and fragrant with the delicious smell of moisture that precedes rain. The only sound she could hear was the roar of the rushing water. She looked out over the valley, amazed at the view. She could even make out the parking area where the ranch truck and trailer stood. The beauty and tranquility made it hard to remember that she was on a very somber mission. If she didn't find Shooting Star soon, she'd have to give up for the day. And then what? She looked at her watch.

"Eek. Starlight. We don't have much time. It's already noon and we're about to get some weather. Dad said no later than twelve thirty, so we better hurry and cover as much ground as we can."

Starlight raised his head from where he was quietly nibbling grass along the edge of the stream. She had just put the bridle on him when he raised his head and looked up the path. Miranda quickly tightened the cinch and mounted. Starlight splashed through the creek without waiting for Miranda's cue. "What is it, boy? What do you see or hear?"

The trail steepened and made a sharp switchback. Starlight lunged upward, pulling hard with each step. Miranda noticed snowflakes swirling in the air as a cold wind struck her face. In only minutes the flakes grew larger and she could hardly see the trail in front of her.

She wondered if she should turn around, but Starlight seemed to know something, and she didn't want to stop him. She thought he must sense his daughter's presence.

A powerful force knocked her sideways as a searing pain stabbed her left thigh, just before the unmistakable crack of a gunshot. Starlight leapt sideways, twisting in the air. Miranda fell. Her head struck something hard, and everything went black.

Chapter Ten

Miranda opened her eyes, but closed them again quickly to ease the throbbing in her head. She tried to move and pain shot through her leg, bringing tears to her eyes. She opened her eyes again, more slowly. The light was so dim and blurry that she wondered if she had lost her eyesight. She remembered falling, but nothing after that. But her leg! Had there really been a gunshot? She tried to figure out where she was lying. She didn't feel any snow. Was she buried in it?

She jumped when something touched her leg, sending another searing pain through her body.

"Don't move."

Miranda tried to sit up to see who was talking—and regretted it. She groaned and lay still.

"I made a poultice. I'm putting it on the holes in your leg. I'm sorry I had to cut your jeans to get to both sides. I'll use a strip to hold the poultices in place."

"Who are you? Where am I?" Miranda asked as her eyes became accustomed to the dim light. Rosy shadows flickered on a rough gray wall.

"I'm Teddy Hungry Horse. You're in my cave. Actually, it's not mine. I'm just borrowing it from the Awakkulé." A young boy's face appeared above her. It was too dark to see him clearly, but his face seemed smudged with soot. Long dark hair fell over his shoulders. She was sure she must be dreaming.

"Are you real?"

"Yes," he said, as if it were not a foolish question.

"And you're alive?" she asked. "Teddy Hungry Horse?"

"Yes," he said looking at her with raised eyebrows, as if thinking she was a little slow in the head.

"Then I'm alive, too." Miranda paused a moment. "Right?"

"Yes."

Miranda gave a short laugh and said, "I wasn't sure. It's all so—weird. I thought I might be dreaming."

When the boy didn't answer she said, "I don't know how I got here. I don't know where here is."

Teddy didn't answer as he put more wood on the fire, which Miranda saw clearly for the first time. It was the source of the flickering light.

"What happened to me?" she asked as she tried to move her leg, sending pain through her body.

"Somebody shot you—in the leg." He leaned over her as he added, "It wasn't me."

"Please tell me where I am and how I got here," Miranda, overwhelmed with fear and pain, shuddered.

"I brought you here, to this cave. I had help from the Awakkulé and Rising Sun."

Miranda had no idea who Awakkulé and Rising Sun were, but she was glad Teddy had help and was not all alone as his grandmother had thought. It explained how he survived. Her head swam with thoughts that she couldn't quite form into words. She closed her eyes.

"Ow! That's hot. What are you doing?" She pushed herself up to see him place a steaming cloth against her leg.

"Sorry. It needs to be as hot as you can stand it."

"My jeans. What did you do?"

"You have a hole all the way through your leg. I couldn't get to it without cutting the leg off your jeans. I'm using the cloth from it for a poultice to draw out any poison from the bullet."

"A bullet went through my leg?" Miranda stared at the denim dressings, one on each side of her leg as the boy used another strip to hold them in place. As her head cleared, all that Teddy had been telling her gradually began making sense.

"Starlight!" she said, remembering. "Where is my horse? I remember. I was riding Starlight. We were looking for you and Shooting Star. If the bullet went through my leg it must have gone into him. Right about where his heart and lungs would be. He could be dead. Is he dead? Where is my horse?" She was talking so fast in near hysterics that the boy sat back on his haunches again and stared at her.

Miranda stared back, her anger growing. "I should say horses. Did you steal my horse? If you are Teddy Hungry Horse, your grandmother thinks you did. What have you done with Shooting Star? If you know where Starlight is, you'd better answer. Is he dead? Tell me!"

Teddy held up his hand, palm out, silencing her.

Miranda quit talking and stared, waiting.

"Rising Sun let me know that someone was near, so I let her lead me down the mountain. I heard a gunshot, and then I heard a horse squeal. I saw a dark horse disappear into the trees. Then I saw you on the ground. I thought you were dead. But when I got to you, I felt your heart. It was beating. I could see you were breathing, but I couldn't make you wake up. Your head was bleeding where it hit the rock."

Miranda's hand flew to the back of her head. Her hair was stiff and matted with dried blood.

"I looked around for the shooter. A deer hunter, maybe. Maybe someone thought you were an elk or a deer. I never saw anyone, and no one came to help."

"So how did you get me here?"

"I lifted you onto Rising Sun's back. Then I got on, too, so you wouldn't fall off. She carried us back here to our cave. She knew the way even though it was snowing so hard I couldn't see."

"Rising Sun is a horse? I thought you were talking about a man."

"Not a man. My horse."

"Do you mean my horse? What color is she? Where is she now?" Miranda rose up on her elbows and looked around the cave. She saw the silhouette of a horse against the dim outline of the cave entrance. "Shooting Star. That's my horse!"

"You? You owned Rising Sun?"

"Her name is Shooting Star, and, yes, I own her. I brought her to the fair to race, and you took her. How could you do that? How could you take someone's horse? Don't you know that's stealing?"

"She gave herself to me. The great spirit sent the horse. I think that makes her mine, now."

"Yeah?" Miranda spit the word. "We'll see about that. I wonder if they put ten-year-old boys in jail."

Teddy rose and walked to the fire. He picked up a branch from a pile and stirred it.

Miranda's anger melted away as grief mingled with pain and brought tears to her eyes and a sob to her throat. The boy had saved her life, and she was yelling at him, threatening prosecution. Her beloved Starlight was lost or dead somewhere in this awful storm. She tried not to cry, but she couldn't stop. Suddenly it was all so overwhelming, she couldn't stand it.

Her father would be frantic when she didn't show up. Was he out looking for her in the storm? What if he died in the blizzard? Miranda wanted her mother and her own warm bed. She shivered as she wondered if she'd ever see her family again. Would the boys be sad again? She'd promised not to scare them by staying away. Tears streamed down her face, and she didn't have the energy to wipe them away.

She felt a blanket cover her. Teddy leaned over her, concern in his eyes. "I will let you have Rising Sun. She will take you back to safety when the storm is over."

Miranda had a million questions for Teddy. But not now. She couldn't sort them out. She couldn't get words past her throat. With Teddy sitting beside her wiping her tears with his thumb, she sank into a deep sleep.

Dreams of men with guns shooting at her, shooting

Starlight, hanging him in a tree and gutting him, just as she'd seen her grandfather and her uncle do with deer they'd shot. When Miranda approached, one of them turned to her with an evil snarl. "Thanks for coming, missy. You are next, you know." It was Hicks, the man who'd tried to kill Starlight once before. Now he'd done it, and he was about to kill her, too. Or so her terrifying dream would have it.

Chapter Eleven

She awakened with a start. Her whole body and her head hurt. She was stiff and sore from lying on the hard ground. The fire was out. Just a few smoldering coals winked from the dark ashes. She had to pee so badly it hurt. She rolled onto her side, pain shooting through her leg and her head. She managed to get to her hands and knees.

Teddy was immediately at her side. "Do you need help?"

"I have to go outside."

"I think you should lie still."

"I can't. I have to pee."

"Okay. Use me to pull yourself up, but try not to put weight on your hurt leg. Lean on me, like a crutch."

Miranda did as he said and limped to the cave entrance. A snowdrift blocked the way.

"Here. On this side there's a path between the rock wall and the drift. Hold on to the rock and then that tree. I'll wait here."

The air was cold. A very narrow path was made by horse hooves and little boy feet. Miranda edged around a corner and relieved herself as quickly as possible. It was still snowing, but the wind had abated. The light was too dim for her to see her watch.

As she edged back, she tripped and fell face first into the snow. "Ouch!" she yelled as her bare left leg sank into the snow, the coldness of it taking her breath away. But it seemed to take away some of the pain, too.

Teddy stood beside her, helping her up. She leaned on him again as he led her back inside. A fire blazed again from the pit in the middle of the floor. Smoke filled the room, and Miranda coughed.

"Sorry about the smoke," Teddy said. "There is a natural chimney, but the air is so heavy it's not allowing the smoke to get out. It will when the fire gets hotter."

Miranda looked up to see a small fissure in the rock where a bit of light came through. "Is it morning?" she asked, sitting in front of the fire.

"Yes. I am making breakfast for you."

"Teddy, I'm sorry I yelled at you. You saved my life. I should be thanking you for taking care of me."

He nodded. "I need to make another poultice."

"First, let's make a sort of ice pack with snow. I think that will numb the pain.

"Okay." Teddy picked up the denim wrap and went to the entrance to fill it with snow.

Miranda held it first to the outside of her leg, and then the inside, shivering, but glad to feel the relief from the pain as her leg became somewhat numb. Teddy put the blanket over her shoulders. She wrapped it around her legs, too, and thanked him.

She looked around. "Where is Shooting Star?"

"Axxaashe Chile went out to find food. She will return. She always does."

"Is that how you say Shooting Star in Crow?"

"In Apsáalooke, which is what we call our language, it means, 'the sun is rising.' She is the color of the rising sun, so that is what I call her."

"How did you get her here? And why? Why did you run away? Were you counting coup. I've heard that stealing an enemy's horse will earn a young man a feather."

"You ask too many questions at once."

"Okay, first. Why did you run away?"

"Two reasons. I wanted to hide from my father when I heard he was out of jail. I didn't want him to take me away from my grandmother. That is one reason. The other one is more important. It was time for me to fast and pray and learn the right way to live." He took a deep breath and went on. "I didn't know if the Great Creator was guiding me to go at this exact time. But then, as I was walking home from the pow wow, I saw the horse. I prayed, "Akbaatatdia, if it gives itself to me I will know that you mean I am to go now."

"What does Akbaat—whatever you said. What does it mean?

"God. The One who created everything."

"So then you stole my horse?"

"I didn't steal her. She gave herself to me."

"How?"

"It was late at night when I saw her. I was coming home from dancing in the arbor when I met her. She stood there, waiting for me. She let me pet her. She knew me."

"How could she?"

"Our spirits recognized each other." Teddy frowned and continued. "I went to my house and got camping supplies. I couldn't tell grandmother, for she would have stopped me, but I knew it was time. Grandmother wasn't home yet, so I put on a winter jacket, even though the night was plenty warm, and left. I wore a full back pack with a sleeping bag and blanket tied to it. I carried a small rope to make a bridle." Teddy looked at Miranda.

"Go on."

"I saw her again—loose. Like she was just waiting for me. I spoke to her in my language. I said..." and the words that came from Teddy's mouth, spoken with his eyes closed, sounded very strange to Miranda. They whooshed and halted and stuttered and sang.

"What does that mean?"

"I was telling her that if she came to me, it was a sign from Akbaatatdia that she was meant to take me to the mountains to get a vision so that I would know my path."

"And she came to you?"

"She stood there watching me, and I walked to her and petted her and put the rope around her neck and nose like a halter. 'Close enough,' I thought, and I led her down by the river where I found a rock to stand on so I could get on her."

"And she just stood there, letting you get on?" Miranda found that hard to believe, knowing Shooting Star's habit of taking off before the rider was ready.

"Yes. Maybe another sign from God?"

"Shooting Star is young and flighty. She spooks at the littlest things. I'm surprised she didn't dump you."

"Don't be surprised. A gift from the spirit world is not going to hurt me. You should know that."

Miranda rolled her eyes and sighed. "This is a very long way from Crow Agency. How did you come so far without getting caught?"

"First, I crossed the Little Bighorn River there at the watering hole and went into the willows..."

"You got Star to cross the river?" Miranda found that even harder to believe. Maybe it wasn't her horse after all.

"Yes. Do you want me to tell you my story?"

"Sure. Sorry. Go on."

"On the other side of the river, it was quiet. People were either sleeping or still at the dances. I saw no one as I left town. We stayed on the road that goes under the interstate toward these mountains. I've been that way many times in my uncles' car, but it seems much longer by horseback. It took me seven days. I could have made it in less, but we were in no hurry. Sometimes we traveled long hours through hot sun and through rain because there were no watering holes or trees for shelter. But when possible, I rode in the very early mornings before sunup and rested in the afternoon and evening when the day was hottest. We rested whenever we found watering holes and shade."

Teddy paused to stir the fire.

"When we got to the Bighorn River," he said, "we stayed a couple of days. Maybe more. There were trees for shade, good grass for Rising Sun. I had plenty to eat, too. I caught a snake and also killed a rabbit to cook over my fire under the bridge."

Miranda was about to say something about eating a snake, when Teddy continued. "We both liked the water to keep us cool during the day. We found a good swimming hole."

"You got Star to get in the water? Surely she didn't swim in the river with you." Miranda thought she knew Shooting Star better than that. She couldn't believe that she'd step into the river for anyone.

"She liked the water. I would ride her into the river, and when it got nice and deep, I stood on her back and dove in. We did it over and over again."

Miranda shook her head in disbelief.

"Didn't anyone pass you on the road or stop to question you?"

"People in cars passed me. But no one stopped. I was not breaking any law." Teddy stopped for a moment and he turned the slab of meat he held over the fire. The smell of it cooking made Miranda's mouth water.

"I thought Grandmother might come looking for me," Teddy continued, "but I prayed she wouldn't."

"She thought your father kidnapped you. She was so sure of it, she was only looking for a way to find him."

"See? I had good reason to fear my father."

"Well, he's back in jail. Did you know that?"

"No. I planned to stay here until Akbaatatdia gave me a sign that it was safe to return. I guess he sent you to tell me."

"Answer my other question—about counting coup by stealing my horse."

"I told you, I did not steal your horse. You are not my enemy, and the horse was free, not in your possession. So taking her would not be counting coup. She was given to me."

Miranda sighed. How could she argue? Everything he'd told her about Shooting Star seemed contrary to her nature, yet here he was, and she wanted to believe it was her horse that had brought him here.

"What is that you are cooking? Smells good."

"Rabbit. I shot it yesterday before the storm. I was almost out of the jerky I made from the deer I killed two days after I came here. I've killed a few rabbits and squirrels also."

"You killed a deer? With what?"

"My bow and arrows. The Awakkulé helped me bring it to this cave. Before, I was just sleeping under the trees. I made the bed you slept on from the deerskin."

Miranda glanced at the place near the fire where she'd spent the night. A deer hide lay flat on the floor. Looking back at Teddy, she asked. "Where is Awakkulé now? Does he stay here with you?"

"No, not he. They. Awakkulé are Little People. These mountains are their home. They guard this place against people who come here with bad intentions. Some people say they have sharp teeth like wolves and they sometimes eat people. But to me, they are helpers and friends. My people honor them with gifts whenever they come here. Unless you mean to harm their home, they leave you alone. If they choose your friendship, they will help you, give you visions, and share everything they have."

"So they decided you were a friend, I guess."

"Yes."

Miranda looked warily around the cave. "Where are they—the Little People?"

"Oh, you probably won't see them. They are kind of shy so they hide themselves. But they see you. They might play tricks on you, but they won't hurt you. They always know what people are doing on their mountain."

"I didn't give them any gift."

"Maybe you did. Maybe you gave them your black horse."

"Don't say that! Starlight's mine, and he's got to be all right. He's my best friend and *my* helper. He saved my life once."

"Then he is probably fine. Maybe the Awakkulé are watching out for him, too. I think you came as a messenger. The Little People are kind to you."

Ordinarily, Miranda would have scoffed at the idea of little people, like elves or leprechauns. But in this eerie cave with a boy who seemed to perform impossible feats for a ten-year-old, she thought it must be true. Silently she thanked the Little People and prayed they'd bring Starlight.

"Here. Drink this." Teddy handed Miranda a cup in which he'd just poured a purplish liquid from a pan on a rock next to the fire.

"What is it?"

"Tea. It's good for you. It'll help your body fight infections that could come from your wound. It'll get rid of the swelling in your leg."

Miranda sipped it cautiously. "Oohh. It's bitter. Horrible. I can't drink this!"

"Can't?" Teddy frowned. "It's a decision. Anyone can drink it. Do you want to get strong or be sick? Your choice."

"What's it made of?"

"Juniper berries."

"Aren't they poison?"

"No, they are good medicine. I know these things. My grandmother teaches me, and I read books."

Miranda remembered a rule about wild berries that her dad had taught her. "Black or blue berries are never poisonous. Red berries can go either way, but never eat a white or yellow berry. They will kill you." Well, if what he said was true, the blue juniper berries were safe even though they'd been so bitter she didn't think they were fit to eat. She forced herself to drink, but very slowly. By the end of the cup, it was getting easier to get down.

"I made the poultice by crushing juniper berries and mixing them with ashes from the fire and a bit of hot water. I think it will help. We'll do it again after I gather more dry berries."

Teddy handed her the piece of meat he'd just cooked. She bit into it cautiously. It tasted very good.

As Teddy cooked another piece for himself, she asked, "So, what kind of peace offering did you give to the Little People?"

"I shot my arrows ahead of me so they'd recognize me. Then when I brought down a deer, I gave the first one to them."

"You saw them?"

"Just a glimpse. More like shadows. I felt them."

"And they took the deer?"

"In the morning it was gone."

"So you shot a second deer, and they helped you bring it here?"

Teddy nodded.

Miranda didn't think Teddy was lying, but she thought he had a great imagination. A mountain lion or even a hunter could have found the dead deer and dragged it away. How he lifted the deer onto Star's back, she couldn't imagine. How she would have let him was a bigger mystery. He must have a special way with horses. Or maybe the Awakkulé had really helped.

"So, you came here to get a vision? Did you get any answers?"

"I did."

"What?"

"I will not tell you. The secrets are sacred and meant only for me and my people." Teddy shrugged an apology, and went on. "One night when I was very hungry and cold, I had a hard time falling asleep, but when I did, I was given a dream. It was the dream I was looking for. And I didn't have to cut off my finger to get it as the great chief did when he was eleven."

"What!" Miranda wasn't sure she'd heard correctly. An eleven-year-old boy cut off his finger? Why?"

"Just the end of his finger, to draw blood. It had worked for other men, and he wanted a dream to tell him the future of his tribe," Teddy smiled. "It worked. All his predictions came true. He was a very brave warrior and a wise chief."

Miranda stared at him, wide eyed. Even though everything he said sounded a like a fairy tale, she still believed he was as honest as Elliot or Kort, who she knew would never intentionally tell a lie. Thinking of the boys made her terribly homesick and full of concern for her family.

"We've got to get down the mountain. My father and your grandmother are probably worried sick. They'll be looking for us."

"You cannot walk. We must wait for the horses."

"Like they are just going to show up here? We need to go looking for them."

Teddy lay down the piece of meat he had been chewing on, closed his eyes, raised his head, and folded his hands. He spoke in the strange sounding language and then softly sang an eerie song, his voice rising in pitch and increasing in cadence.

Miranda stared at him until at last he opened his eyes and said, "We wait here. The horses will come. Two of them. One red and one black. They'll come tomorrow when the storm is gone and the sun shines high in the blue sky. We will wait until then."

Miranda nodded. She hoped Teddy was right. Feeling too tired to move very far, she was okay with waiting. She eyed the deerskin. "I took your bed."

"It's yours, now."

"Thank you. I want to lie down, now. My leg is throbbing."

"I'll make another poultice, but first I must go find more berries." Teddy put more wood on the fire and left.

Miranda made a pillow of her coat and pulled the blanket over her shoulders. Before taking the long ride back down the mountain, she'd need to find a way to cover her leg. Teddy had cut the left leg of her jeans off from about eight inches above her knee. She shuddered to think about his knife cutting through the heavy denim that close to her skin, yet he'd managed not to cut her, not even a scratch. She was glad she'd been unconscious. She thought of how silly she must look in half cut-offs and cowboy boots. Thinking of her boots, she decided to take them off. Her feet were cold and cramped. She sat up, threw back the blanket, and reached for her boot.

She had to twist a little sideways to look at the wound. The bullet had entered the fleshy part of her leg near the back and gone straight through, coming out the other side. The skin around both holes in her leg was red and swollen, but there wasn't any sign that there had been much bleeding. The bullet had obviously missed the bone. It would have missed her completely if it had been an inch or two farther back. What would it have done to Starlight? Probably killed him. Had it? Or had her leg slowed it down enough to save her horse. Maybe. Teddy seemed so sure that Starlight was all right. She'd have to wait until tomorrow to see.

It hurt too much to tug on her boots, so she gave up and lay back on the deerskin, pulled the blanket over her shoulder, and tucked it under her chin. She wished Teddy would come back. She could hear wind whistling outside the cave. The entrance revealed nothing but white with no difference between snow covered ground and sky. She shivered. Staring at the fire, she gradually relaxed and finally fell asleep.

She dreamed that Little People—men and women about two or three feet tall—danced around her. At first she was afraid, but when a child, about half that tall, placed a soothing hand on her forehead and began to sing in a soft and beautiful voice in a language that Miranda didn't know, her fear left her. Her body warmed. Miranda saw herself rising. Not standing, but floating toward the ceiling of the cave. She felt herself slide through the space between the rocks where the smoke from the fire escaped. She floated upward as if she were smoke.

She looked down. Little People were everywhere, some working, some hiding behind rocks. Some pointing up at her. She floated down to a little valley that was warm and green. Children of the Little People played on a carpet of flower-studded grass. They were adorable and waved to her as she floated by. She saw a horse. A black one. She flew to it, calling, "Starlight, Starlight!" But when she reached out to touch its nose, it changed into a man, bigger than a horse. His face looked just like Hicks's until he opened his mouth to reveal rows and rows of shark's teeth. Miranda screamed.

"Sorry!" Teddy said. "Did I hurt you?"

Miranda's eyes flew open, and she looked up into Teddy's kind face. She was back in the cave, lying on the deerskin. "I had a terrible dream."

"My grandmother calls them fever dreams. They are the worst!"

"I have fever?"

"Yes. I must put another poultice on your leg. I have it ready. Okay?"

Miranda's cheeks burned and her mouth was dry. Her headache was back. When Teddy applied the hot poultice to her leg, she didn't even cringe. It felt good. She couldn't get warm enough. She shook with chills. "I am so cold."

Teddy laid a sleeping bag over the blanket that covered her. "I won't need this right now," he said. "Maybe you can sleep again. It is good for healing."

"Oh, I don't want to go to sleep. The dreams are terrible. Would you just stay and talk to me?"

"Okay." But Teddy remained quiet.

"Tell me why you came here—besides to hide from your father. Do all Crow boys go on vision quests?"

"I do not know what they all do. Some Apsáalooke children have forgotten the way of our ancestors. White men have taken much away from us. We no longer have a chief. We haven't since the death of the great one. I want to change that. I want to be a chief like he was."

"Who was he?"

"You don't know about the last Apsáalooke chief?"

"No. They don't exactly teach that in my school."

Miranda assumed, though, that he was talking about Chief Plenty Coups as his grandmother had mentioned. She wanted to know more about him.

"I will not speak his name because it is sacred."

"Why is it sacred?" Miranda asked.

"Because he is gone to be with Akbaatadia. When someone dies and goes to be with the Creator, he becomes sacred, too." Teddy looked into her face with great intensity. "I learned that from reading all about the great chief. Not all Apsáalooke still follow that rule."

"Why don't you just say, 'Crow'?" Miranda asked. You say most things in English."

"Crow is the name the white man gave us because he misunderstood what Apsáalooke means."

"What does it mean?"

"Children of the large-beaked bird."

"What bird?"

"I believe it's the raven, cousin to the crow, but I like saying the Apsáalooke name better."

"Oh. I'll try to say it like you do, then."

"Now, I will tell you about the chief. Then you can understand why I came here. It is because I want to follow in his footsteps as much as it is possible.

"He went to the mountains, and Awakkulé spoke to him when he was just nine years old. What they told him made him happy. He knew he would be a chief. When he was eleven, like I told you, he went to the mountains again, the Crazy Mountains, and received a vision of what was to come to our people. And it all came true. He became a chief when he was twenty-eight and was chief until he died when he was more than eighty. He was very wise. He told his people they must study and learn or the white people would rule them. But with education, we are their equal, he said. I will study everything I can, but mostly I study the lessons of this great chief. I *am* like him. The Awakkulé helped him and spoke to him. And they have spoken to me and helped me."

"Can't you tell me anything that they told you?"

"I told you that the horses will appear tomorrow."

"What have they told you about me?"

"That you are good, and they would help you."

"What about later? What will happen when I get back home? Will my horses be okay? Can you find out if the man, Hicks, is going to come after me or my horses?"

"That is not my life. I can only have visions about my life. You must have your own vision and pay attention. If you don't believe them, your dreams won't come true."

"Are you afraid of your dad?"

"No, but I don't want to live with him."

"Why?"

"He has drifted far away from Apsáalooke ways. He lives for money. Some kids at school told me he stole money from the tribal council. I know it's true—lots of money. It was in the newspaper."

"What happened to your mother? Why don't you live with her?"

"She couldn't take living with my father, especially when he drank alcohol, so she left. I don't know any more than that. Grandmother does, but she will not say bad things about my parents to me."

As more chills shook Miranda's body, she pulled the blanket tighter around her shoulders. She nearly drifted off to sleep, but woke herself, for fear of having more nightmares.

"Try to go to sleep," Teddy ordered. "It is many hours before the storm quits and the horses return."

Miranda closed her eyes and drifted into a dream inhabited by Little People riding horses in the sky, shooting arrows at her as she tried to hide behind rocks and trees. But, then she noticed that the arrows were flying above her head. She turned to look. It was the big one that looked like Hicks—the one with sharks' teeth. Maybe the Little People were not shooting at her, but protecting her, instead.

When she awakened she wondered about her dream. Did it foretell her future? Was Hicks looking for her? Would the Awakkulé save her from him?

Chapter Twelve

The day and night that followed were filled with alternating nightmares and searing pain, headache, and chills. Miranda lay still, drifting in and out of sleep, her eyes tightly closed. Whenever she opened them, she saw only the flickering red glow from the fire dancing on the dark limestone walls. Occasionally, she heard Teddy stir the fire and throw on more wood. She hardly felt the hot compresses he applied to her leg. When the coldness of fresh snow touched her, she opened her eyes and mouthed "thank you" to the boy who crouched beside her, before drifting off again.

Teddy urged her to sip more juniper tea, but she drank little, asking instead for water. He melted snow and offered her drinks at intervals. She sipped the water and then sank back into delirium. When at last she awakened, soaked in sweat, she pushed the blanket away.

"I'm so hot!" she murmured.

"Your fever has broken," Teddy said, smiling. "And someone is here to see you."

Miranda closed her eyes, her mind drifting, remembering when she had awakened in another cave when she was about Teddy's age. Her grandparents, Mr. Taylor, and Elliot had found her. The memory became a happy dream as she sank back into a dazed sleep—until the clip, clop of iron shoes on stone roused her, again. She opened her eyes and rose to her elbows.

"Starlight! You did come back." She rolled to her side, grasped a stirrup and pulled herself up, standing on her right foot. "You're alive. Are you hurt?"

"Rising Sun found your black horse and led him here. I knew she would," Teddy said proudly. "I don't think he is hurt." He pointed to a hole near the top of the left fender of her saddle. Dried blood was spattered and smeared around the hole. "Look underneath," he said.

She lifted the stirrup and hooked it over the horn. The lower edge of the D-ring that the latigo fastened to was dented, evidence that the bullet had gone no farther. Miranda unfastened the cinch, and Teddy helped her lower the saddle to the ground. She carefully examined Starlight's side. She saw nothing but smooth black hair, slightly ruffled from the saddle. Starlight was unhurt.

"If we are to leave today, we should start or we will not get down the mountain before dark."

Miranda looked at the cave opening. The snow was dazzling white, and the sky bright blue. She looked at her watch. One twenty.

With Teddy's help, she managed to slide the saddle onto Starlight's back without putting weight on her left leg. After standing for so long, it ached more than ever. She wanted to lie down and go to sleep to escape the pain, but she wanted more to get back to her family.

She reached for the reins of the bridle he still wore over his halter and noticed that one was missing. She tied the end of the remaining rein onto the empty ring of the bit, and looped it over his head. "Good boy, Starlight. I wish you could tell me where you've been and what you've done and what you've seen. I wish we could find the person who tried to kill you."

Teddy gathered his belongings into his backpack and rolled the blanket and sleeping bag into the deerskin.

"Do you want to tie that roll behind Starlight's saddle? We can use his halter rope. You don't have a saddle for Star or any way to hold it on her."

Teddy nodded. He used the rope to secure the bedroll, so it wouldn't unfurl. The roll was heavy, and Miranda helped lift it onto the tall horse and tied it down with the saddle strings. She slowly lowered herself to the ground, suddenly too exhausted to hold her own weight. She didn't think she had the strength to mount her horse.

"What's wrong," Teddy asked. "We need to go."

"I just need to rest a minute," Miranda said. "I don't think I could even get on now. I'd just fall off."

"Then perhaps we should wait until tomorrow."

Miranda thought about her parents' anguish. She couldn't bear to make them wait any longer. She couldn't bear to wait any longer to see them. "I'll be good to go if I can rest just ten minutes." She lay back on the ground, welcoming the firm support.

"Okay. While you rest, let me wrap your leg. You'll freeze out there without it covered." Teddy pulled a long-sleeved T-shirt from his coat pocket. He put one sleeve inside the other and told Miranda to take off her boot and slip her foot into the doubled shirtsleeve.

"You pull off my boot. I can't."

Teddy did so and guided her foot into the sleeves. When the bottom of the makeshift legging reached the top of her sock, he stopped and wrapped the rest of the shirt around her leg, over the denim bandage that still covered the wound and up to where it met the cut-off leg of her jeans. He tied the shirt on with a rope made of braided grass. "Now, try to keep what's left of your jeans over the top of the shirt so it covers all your skin."

"Thanks. I'm getting cold lying here. Can you help me get on Starlight?" Miranda asked.

She donned her knit cap and leather gloves, grabbed the saddle horn, and tried to lift her left leg to the stirrup. Hot pain stabbed her at the site of the wound. "That won't work. I'll have to get on the other side." With a big boost from Teddy, she managed to pull herself up in the stirrup and ease her left leg over the saddle and settle into it. "Thanks. Now, if I can just stay on. Please go slow."

The horses picked their way down the mountain. Teddy, on Shooting Star, led the way with Starlight walking gingerly behind her. It was as if he knew his rider was holding on to the saddle horn to brace herself against every jolt and to keep from falling off. She didn't touch the rein. Every once in a while Starlight's feet would slip a little in the snow causing Miranda to open her eyes, gasp, and tighten her hold. She'd never felt this fearful or unsteady on a horse before. Once or twice when the ground leveled out for a ways, she nodded off into a light doze and then awoke with a jerk. She didn't remember the ride up the mountain being this far. The sun was edging toward the horizon when Teddy stopped and said, "This is where I found you."

Miranda stared at the spot and groaned. It had taken her half a day to get that far when she came up the mountain. It would take them half the night to get back, if they made it at all. She wanted to cry.

Teddy looked at her. "Don't worry. The Awakkulé guide us. We'll get back safely."

Miranda could barely keep from crying. She was worn out, cold to the bone, and getting colder as the sun slipped behind a cloud. Her leg and her whole body ached, but she nodded and cued Starlight to go on.

After what seemed like an hour, but must have been only a few minutes, she recognized the place where she'd eaten lunch and crossed the stream. What a long way yet to go, she thought, and her shoulders sagged. She thought she heard music. Slowly she relaxed, willed herself not to think of the distance yet to travel, but to hold on and trust Starlight to take her home. As she rode along with her eyes closed, she slowly realized that the music was coming from Teddy. He was singing in his native tongue. Somehow the sound gave her courage.

Darkness came quickly, and Miranda wondered how the horses knew where to step. It wasn't long, however, before a full moon peeked over the eastern horizon and lit the path they were following. It was a better trail than Miranda had used coming up. Longer with lots of switchbacks, but not so steep and rocky. By the time they reached level ground the moon was high in the sky and Miranda's spirits had risen with it. "I don't think it's much farther, if Dad and your grandma are still where we left the pickups and trailers."

"If not, we can still make it to Pryor by morning," Teddy said.

What a discouraging thought! *You just have to be there, Daddy,* she said to herself.

It had been a long time since Miranda had been able to feel anything but pain in her toes. She was so cold that she feared hypothermia would kill her before they could ride another mile. She gritted her teeth, held on, and let Starlight take her across the ravine.

"Do you think we could go a little faster now?" Teddy asked. "Rising Sun wants to run."

"I could try. Starlight's pretty smooth." Miranda gathered the rein in her numb hand and let him pick up the pace behind his daughter who'd stretched into a smooth trot. The wind in her face chilled Miranda, but the added motion seemed to put some blood back into her muscles. She closed her eyes tight and held on, willing herself to be strong.

She heard a prolonged whinny in the distance. Starlight answered with a neigh that shook his whole body. Miranda laughed out of sheer relief.

"Queen!" she shouted.

She heard a car door slam just after she saw a flash of interior lights. Soon she could see the silhouette of the truck and trailer and a man getting on a horse. All three horses called to each other again. Queen raced toward them, quickly closing the distance between them until she could see her father's face in the moonlight.

He jumped off Queen as she skidded to a stop. As he reached for Miranda, she fell into his arms and sobbed. "Oh, Daddy. I'm so glad to see you. I didn't know if we would make it."

Dad hugged her tight. "Oh, Mandy, my baby. I've never been so glad to see anyone in my life! I was afraid we'd never find you alive after that blizzard!"

When he set her down, her legs buckled. He grabbed her and picked her up again. "Baby, you're hurt!" He carried her as he led the two horses back to the truck. He started the engine and put Miranda in the front seat. He told Teddy to get in, too. "You're freezing, son. I'll take care of the horses."

The cab of the pickup was warm and getting warmer. Both Miranda and Teddy shivered. As her feet began to thaw, pain returned to her toes and spread up her legs. She bit her lip and squeezed her eyes shut. "I've never been this cold," she groaned.

"Me, either," Teddy said, and a sob escaped him.

Headlights appeared and grew larger until Lucille's pickup and trailer pulled to a stop beside them. Teddy jumped out and ran into his grandmother's arms. "How did you know I was here?" he asked after she made sure he was all right.

"I woke up from a dream about you and had a strong feeling that I needed to get back here. I was sleeping at a friend's house in Pryor."

Dad, Miranda, Teddy, and Lucille all crowded together in the warm cab of Dad's truck. They talked for a long time as the children warmed up and told their stories. When both earth and sky took on a rosy hue, Miranda looked to the east. The sky was red with streaks of brilliant gold. *I made it to morning*, she thought. She had truly feared that she would never see the sun or feel warm again.

"We've got to get you to a hospital, Mandy. I'll load the horses and drive you to Billings."

Lucille and Teddy got out with Dad, leaving Miranda alone in the cab. She had to tell Teddy goodbye, so she got out, too, and hobbled around the pickup, using it for support. Teddy was leaning on Shooting Star, his arms around her, talking in Crow.

He finally stepped back, and Dad led the filly into the trailer beside Queen.

"How is Queen's leg?" Miranda asked. "I didn't see her limping."

"I think it's going to be fine. I've been riding her all afternoon, looking for you. I think it bled enough to keep out any infection, but I keep it wrapped."

Teddy touched her arm and she turned to him. "Goodbye, Teddy. Thank you for saving my life. You can come visit any time. I know Star would like that and so would I."

Teddy said something in his language. She guessed it was goodbye, but she didn't know. She waved as he and his grandma got in her pickup and drove away.

"What are you doing out here in the cold?" Dad

asked, gently scolding her. "You have to stay off that leg."

"I had to say goodbye to Teddy. He saved my life, Dad."

"Thank heavens for that!" Her father said, as he carried her to the truck. "We'll have to find some way to show our gratitude. There is no way we can ever repay him. Now, buckle up, Mandy. We're taking you to a doctor before you do any more damage to your leg."

Chapter Thirteen

Miranda's leg throbbed and her head pounded. She could not get comfortable on the narrow bed in the Billings Clinic emergency room. She just wanted to get the horses safely home, crawl into her own soft bed, and let her mom take care of her.

A white-haired man in a white coat strode into the room, frowning as he slapped x-ray images on the back-lit white board on the wall.

"We need to get her into surgery ASAP," he said, looking at Dad. "We have a slot open just before noon. That'll give us time to get her admitted and prepped." He paused, extended his hand to Dad, and said, "I'm Dr. White, by the way."

Of course, Miranda thought. *And I'm right here, and I'm not deaf or dead yet.*

"What did you find?" Dad squinted at the images.

Dr. White removed a pen from his pocket and used it as a pointer. "Hard to tell on an x-ray, but I suspect these darker spots are from foreign material, and that is what is causing the infection. They will need to be removed before we can get rid of the infection."

"Well, then, we better get it done," Dad said

"Surgery? No, wait." Miranda said, or at least she thought she did. But no one seemed to hear.

"We'll get an IV started with antibiotics. We'll operate as soon as the anesthesiologist gets here."

Dad nodded.

"Wait, Dad!" Miranda tried again. "Don't I get a say in what we do to my leg? We have to get the horses home first. We can't leave them standing in the trailer all day. What's to keep someone from stealing them while we're in here. Let's go home first and then take me to a closer hospital."

The doctor looked at Miranda for the first time. "I don't think you want to wait on this. You have signs of sepsis. That's blood poisoning. Your fever is high and so is your heart rate. The reddening and discoloration around the wound show the beginning signs of gangrene. Wait, and we may need to amputate. Wait too long, and it may be too late for even that." Exasperation colored his expression and his voice.

Miranda gulped as she began to realize the seriousness of the situation.

"You will stay here and have the surgery, Miranda. We will not let this go any longer. My God, what if you hadn't made it out of the mountains when you did?"

Dad's voice broke. Miranda was surprised to see tears in his eyes. She nodded and tried not to cry with him, but a sob escaped and tears flowed. This was all too much after what she'd already been through.

Dad put a hand on her shoulder. "Don't worry, baby. We're here where they can take care of you and get you through this. And I'll see that the horses are okay. I know a rancher..." A knock on the door interrupted him and a nurse entered. She handed the doctor a sheet of paper.

"This proves my point," the doctor said. "The lab report confirms a high white count. The infection is bad. Let's get started."

In just minutes from the time he left the room, a man and a woman came in with a tray of medical supplies. He hung a bag of fluids on a pole attached to the head of her bed while she swabbed the back of Miranda's hand and began inserting a needle. Miranda barely felt the prick, closed her eyes, and drifted into a land of horrifying fever dreams.

When she awakened, she was shaken by dreams about Teddy and Rising Sun. *No,* she thought. *He can't call her that. He can't have her.* It took a while to remember the filly's real name. "Shooting Star," she said groggily as she felt a hand on her arm.

"Let me help you raise up just a little, sweetie. We'll get your shirt off and put this on you." Miranda felt her shoulders being lifted, but had no strength to help.

A woman leaned into view. "I'm Dr. Bowman, your anesthesiologist. We're going to give you something in your IV to help you sleep while Dr. White takes care of your leg. Can you count backward for me from ten?"

"Wait! Where's Dad?"

"I'm here, baby. I have a place for the horses. I'll take them while you're in surgery."

"Miranda," Dr. Bowman said. "Count for me. From ten to one."

"Okay, ten," and that was the last she remembered.

She awakened in a different room, and Dad was by her side. So was the grouchy Dr. White. Only this time he was smiling. "Glad to see you awake so soon, young lady. You did very well through the surgery. We debrided the inside of your wound. That means we scraped all the foreign and damaged tissue from inside the bullet hole. What we found were pieces of denim cloth and leather—and some infected and dying tissue. We are treating the infection with strong antibiotics, both locally and intravenously. We'll keep you here in ICU until we get your fever and your blood count under control, but so far your prognosis looks good."

Miranda had only a vague idea of what he was talking about, but something nagged at her. Then she remembered. "Teddy kept putting hot poultices on it. He made them with crushed juniper berries mixed with ashes. Did that cause the infection?"

"No, I'd guess it saved you from a faster progression of the infection. I'm sure it was the pieces of your jeans and chaps that the bullet drilled into your leg that caused the infection." The doctor smiled again. "You'd better thank your friend, Teddy. He may have saved your life."

"That would make the second time." Miranda said.

"Now, to keep that lifesaving trend going, you rest, drink lots of fluids, and do as the nurses tell you." Doctor White actually saluted as he left the room.

"Daddy? Where are the horses?"

"A friend of mine has a small ranch not far from here. He's keeping them for us until we go home. After Mom gets here, I may take them on home. But I don't want to leave until I know you're okay."

"Mom's coming?"

"Of course. She's been worried sick. She started out as soon as she heard you were being admitted."

"What about the kids."

"They're with Grandma and Grandpa. Now you just concern yourself with getting well. Don't worry about anyone else. Not even the horses."

Miranda might have taken that advice if it weren't for the dreams. Everything she had ever worried about tumbled through her mind as she slept. Her horses kept disappearing. Hicks kept sneaking up on her with all kinds of weapons that grew sharp needles that dripped with poison as he approached. She fought him, but always awoke with him laughing in her face as he tossed her over a cliff where dry, bleached buffalo bones lay at the bottom. The fall always awakened her with a jerk, and she'd vow not to go back to sleep, but she felt groggy and lethargic from the pain medication and the fever, which didn't seem to be going away.

The ringing of a telephone fit into her dreams as an alarm that she couldn't reach to turn off. She murmured in her sleep, tried to turn over and winced in pain.

"I'll get it Mandy. Just sleep," she heard Dad say as she sank back into another dream about being trapped in a house that was on fire.

Chapter Fourteen

Miranda woke when her mother's cool hand touched her forehead.

"Oh, Mandy, baby. What have you done? If your horses aren't the death of you, they'll be the death of me."

"What do you mean, Mom? My horse didn't do this. Someone shot me."

"I know. It's a wonder you lived. I was afraid we'd never find you alive. And then when they finally did, you were wounded. The doctors say..." Mom paused. "These kinds of infections are the worst, so just do as you're told and get well!"

"I'll get well, Mom. Do you realize that they were probably trying to kill Starlight? Maybe they thought he was an elk or something, but that bullet was meant for him. I'm glad it was just my leg and not his heart."

"Do you think that's a comfort to me? You're more important than any horse." Mom held Miranda's hand. "I just wish I'd stuck to my guns and forbade you to take any horses to the Crow Fair. Then none of this would have happened."

"I wondered when you were going to say, 'I told you so,'" Miranda growled, pulling her hand free.

"Sorry. I didn't intend to say that. I know that what's done is done, and grousing about it isn't going to change it. You know it's just because I love you so much. I want you well and safe. Is that too much for a mother to ask?"

"I love you, too, Mom, but you need to understand how much I love my horses." Miranda thought for a minute and added. "This might make you mad, but I'm not sorry I went to the Crow Fair. I'm not sorry I met Teddy. He saved my life twice."

"But your life wouldn't have been in danger if he hadn't stolen your horse."

"Yeah. I know. But he was doing what he thought was right, and how do we know it wasn't?"

"Isn't seeing you lying here in intensive care proof enough that it wasn't right?"

"No. It's not proof. We don't know everything. We don't know what might have happened if I hadn't been there. Maybe his father would have kidnapped him if it hadn't been for Shooting Star."

Mom shook her head. "No, I suppose we don't, and I suppose it does no good to argue with my feisty daughter. All I ask is that you get well." Mom stood, kissed Miranda on the forehead, and asked, "Can I get you anything?"

"Water, please."

Mom held the insulated water cup so that Miranda could drink through the straw.

"Are you staying here all night?" Miranda asked.

"You bet I am. I won't leave until they let me take you home. Dad is staying, too, until you're out of ICU."

The night was terrifying with the sound of beeping machines blending with nightmares. Miranda, when she woke from scary dreams, was comforted to see Mom in the recliner next to her bed.

When she awakened late the next morning, a nurse came in to ask how Miranda was feeling. "And here is the newspaper, if you'd like to look at it," she added, handing a fat copy of the Billings Gazette to Mom. Mom perused it as the nurse took Miranda's vital signs. "How's the pain?" the nurse asked.

Miranda shrugged. "Bearable."

The nurse smiled. "Do you want some more pain medication?"

"No, thanks."

"On a scale of one to ten, with ten as the most excruciating pain you can imagine, how do you rate your pain?"

"I don't think it matters, and I'd probably not be accurate. It hurts, but I can stand it."

"But, you don't have to stand it. We want you to rest and heal."

"I don't like the pain medicine. It makes me all fuzzy-headed."

"I need to put a number on your chart. Could you please make an estimate?"

Miranda heaved a sigh. "Seven, I guess."

"Oh, we don't like for it to get that high. It's best to keep it under control, no higher than four."

"I'm the one feeling it, so it's my choice, right?"

"Yes, but..."

"I'd take an Advil, if I could, but no more of that stuff you put in my IV. Okay?"

"I'll see what I can do," she said and left the room.

"Well, it's nice to know I'm not the only one you give trouble to," Mom said. "Don't you think the nurses and doctors know more than you do?"

"Yeah, but they don't know how I feel."

The phone on the bedside table rang. Mom picked it up, said hello, and handed it to Miranda. "That boy's persistent," she said. "This is the third time he's called, and Laurie called twice."

"What boy?" Miranda asked taking the phone.

"What other boy is there?" Mom asked laughing. "I think I'll go find some breakfast while you visit." Mom stood, laid the newspaper on the bedside table, and picked up her purse.

"Hello?"

"Miranda, tell me everything. I can't wait to see you," Chris said, "But Mom won't let me drive to Billings."

Miranda smiled and lay back, happy to hear the sound of his voice. She told him everything that had happened and asked about how things were at home.

When Chris's Mom told him to get off the phone, Miranda sighed and said goodbye. She didn't want to sleep, so she raised the head of the bed and reached for the newspaper.

She leafed through it slowly, looking for something of interest. In local news, the first item told that she and Teddy Hungry Horse had been found. It mentioned that she was in the hospital, but nothing more than that.

They missed the interesting parts of the story, she thought. She was about to turn the page when a picture caught her eye. She pulled it closer and read the article.

A robbery took place at the Town Pump east of Billings Monday morning, just after midnight when the store was deserted of customers. The middle-aged man, caught on security camera and pictured below, shoved a paper bag that he said held a loaded gun in the direction of the clerk, Jenna Smith, age 22. She quoted him as saying, "Give me your money, a big bottle of Diet Coke, and two of them sandwiches in that case over there."

Miss Smith said she went after the items he ordered. He followed, saying, "No funny business." Back at the cash register, Ms. Smith said, "I'll just ring these up for you, and then give you the cash."

"That's good," the man said.

"It comes to $11.49," Ms. Smith told him.

"Okay," he said. "Take it out of the cash your giving me. Just the bills."

She did as he asked her to do, and he left with $172.00, leaving $11.00 and some coins in the till.

Jenna called the police as soon as he was gone. "He seemed really crazy, so I just went along with him," she said. At last report, the police have been unable to find the suspect. Anyone seeing this man, please call the police.

Miranda dropped the newspaper, stunned. There was no question. The man in the picture was Martin Hicks.

Chapter Fifteen

Miranda reached for the call button and punched it three times, hoping that would make someone hurry. She flung the covers back to get out of bed just as her dad walked in the door.

"Whoa, what are you doing? Do you want me to find a nurse?"

"Dad! Where are the horses?"

"Slow down, little one. Did you just have another nightmare?" Her dad gently pushed her back onto the pillow. He pulled the covers up to her chin and asked, "Why are you calling the nurse."

"You can cancel that. It was you I wanted. Our horses are in danger!"

"What are you talking about? I think the pain medicine is messing with your mind."

"No, Dad. Read this." She showed Dad the article.

"Well, I'll be. What the heck brings that lunatic to Montana? How does he manage it?"

"See. He's here. In Billings. He still wants to kill my horses—and me. Maybe he's the one who shot me."

"I doubt that. He couldn't know that you were in the Pryors. He obviously doesn't have the sense God gave... well, I don't want to insult any animals."

"Dad. Where are the horses? When did you last check on them?"

"They're in the trailer in the parking lot. I went to Shepherd and loaded them up this morning. I just stopped here to see you on my way out."

Miranda threw back the covers again. "Can I see them from here? You'd better get back to them before Hicks finds them."

Dad grabbed her by the arm and settled her back in bed. "I got a report from the doctor before I came in, Miranda. He thinks he has the infection under control, but you have to cooperate."

Tears filled Miranda's eyes. She couldn't keep her horses safe, and Dad was the only one she could count on. Why couldn't he see how serious this was?

"Mandy?" Dad's voice was gentle. "I know you're scared. And you have every right to be. This guy hurt you before. The first thing to do is to call the police and tell them who he is, in case they haven't figured it out yet. I'll do that from the truck."

"Thanks, Dad." Miranda touched his hand as a sob escaped her.

"Do you have your cell phone?" Dad asked.

"I don't know where it is. I think I left it in the truck when we started riding. I knew I wouldn't have service in the mountains."

"Well, I'll keep in touch through your mother's phone."

"What about me?" Mom asked from the doorway.

"Good. You're here. I'm going to..."

"Dad," Miranda interrupted. "Please go. I'll explain everything to Mom. And keep calling to let me know what the police say and how the horses are."

"Police?" Mom asked.

"Mandy will explain." Dad kissed his daughter's forehead. "I've gotta go."

Mom stared at the newspaper as Miranda told her everything she and Dad had talked about.

"Oh, my gosh, Mandy. This is the lunatic that almost killed you?"

"Yes, Mom. Laurie told me she heard he'd escaped from a mental hospital in Ohio. The authorities are looking for him because they consider him dangerous. And he is, Mom. I guess he can't get it out of his mind that he needs to get even with me."

"Well, he's obviously not right in the head," Mom said, thumping the newspaper story, "but who knows? He may be canny in other ways. If he is of just one mindset, he may focus every brain cell he has on that one thing. And if that's you, we've got to take every precaution to keep you safe."

Miranda stared at her mom. Of all the people that she had thought would not understand, Mom was at the top of the list. But she was getting it. Mom had been in California, and Miranda was living with her grandparents when Hicks had attacked her and Starlight.

A muffled ringing blared from somewhere. Mom dug through her purse, pulled out her cell phone and asked, "Did you call the police?" She listened as she paced around the small room.

"Well, they'd better send someone up here to guard Mandy. Did you tell them that?" She listened some more and then said goodbye.

"What did he say? Are the horses okay?"

"They are fine. Dad's on his way home with them. He called the police and let them know who this guy is and that there is a manhunt out for him. They are getting hold of the authorities in Ohio."

"Did he ask the police to come here?"

"No. He didn't think about you being in danger here in the hospital. It's the first thing I thought of when you told me who this guy is. I'm going to call them myself."

"Mom, I don't want a cop sitting outside my room. It's the horses I'm worried about."

"Of course it is," Mom said wryly. "That's why you have a mother to worry about you."

Mom made the call, but Miranda could tell she wasn't having much luck convincing the authorities of the danger Miranda was in. "Why else would he come back to Montana? He tried to kill her once before. He has a personal vendetta with her from way back when he worked for a local rancher."

The officer must have questioned why he would want Miranda dead, because Mom went on. "From what Miranda has told me, Hicks blamed her for getting him fired. But I think it's more because he couldn't handle a certain stallion and she could, so he was jealous."

When Mom finally closed her phone, she looked angry. "They said they'd send someone to talk to us as soon as they could free up a detective. The guy was just humoring me. They won't take this seriously."

"Mom, I'm sure I'm safe in the hospital. Don't worry."

A man in white pants and shirt knocked at the door. "Moving time," he said. "Are you ready for a bigger room with a view?"

"What's going on?" Mom asked, moving closer to Miranda .

"The doctor said she's well enough to leave ICU, so we are taking her to a private room."

"Okay, but I'll be right beside her as you move her."

"Fine," the guy said, looking puzzled.

When Miranda was settled in a sunny room, Mom asked, "Is it possible to put a privacy notice or something on her chart? Let the hospital receptionist and everyone know that her room number is not to be given out to anyone?" Mom asked.

"Maybe," the man said, frowning, "I guess you'd have to talk to case management."

In a few minutes another man entered the room with a tray of instruments.

"What are you planning to do?" Mom asked, sounding alarmed.

"The doctor ordered another blood sample," he answered with a surprised look on his face.

"Well, I'd like to see the order and your hospital ID," Mom said.

"You don't believe me? The doctor is still at the nurses station. I'll get him."

"Mom, that wasn't Hicks, if that's what you're thinking," Miranda said when he left the room.

"Well, he looked a little like the guy in the picture, and anyway, Hicks could have hired someone. I'm just playing it safe."

"Is there a problem?" Dr. White asked from the doorway.

"And you are?" Mom asked.

"I'm the surgeon who operated on this girl's leg," Dr. White said, frowning. "And you are?"

"Mom, he's my doctor. Honest." Miranda said.

"Touché," Mom said, extending her hand. "Mrs. Stevens. We've had quite a scare, and I'd rather be safe than sorry."

"I ordered a blood test so I can stay on top of the infection. Do you have a problem with that?"

"No, not as long as I know what treatments are planned for my daughter. I don't like surprises. I need to know that the people who come in to poke needles in her are legitimate and not someone out to kill her."

"You think the bullet to her leg was intentional?" The doctor raised his eyebrows. "That someone was trying to kill her?"

"Maybe. There's a madman on the loose who tried to kill her once before," Mom said.

The frown on his face showed skepticism, but he just asked. "May I send the lab tech back in now?"

"Yes, of course," Mom said

Dr. White left, shaking his head.

"Well, that went well," Mom said, making a face. "I don't think your doctor likes me much."

"You didn't need to worry, Mom."

Mom shrugged. "I don't care if I make enemies, as long as I can keep you safe."

The man from lab stepped back in the room. When he finished drawing blood, Mom said she'd go talk to someone about security.

"May I use your phone, Mom?"

"Sure." She handed it to Miranda. "I'll be back soon."

Miranda called the Bergmans first. Chris answered.

"Chris, you've got to help me!"

"What? Are you okay?" Chris sounded alarmed.

"I'm fine, but listen to this. It's in the *Billings Gazette*. And there's a picture. It's Hicks." Miranda read the newspaper article.

"Hicks? The guy who poisoned my horse?"

"Yes. And tried to kill Starlight and me."

"That's not good!"

"I know. Dad's on his way home with the horses. We've got to keep a close eye on them, Chris. We've got to figure out a way to keep them safe. And I can't do it from here."

"Maybe I could sleep in the barn."

"Would you?"

"I'll try. But you know my folks. I wonder if there is someplace we can hide them. Maybe your dad could put a lock on the stable doors and keep them inside at night. We could get an alarm system set up so, if anyone tried to get in, the sheriff would be notified."

"Wow, Chris. Thanks for thinking that way. You'll have to convince my Dad, but I think he'll do it. But we've got to hurry. Hicks could already be there by now."

Miranda called Laurie next and told her about Hicks as calmly as she could. "Just be careful when you go to take care of your horses. Have someone with you." They talked about Hicks and what he might do, but finally settled down to talk about everything Miranda was missing at school and all the things they'd do when she got back.

"Hurry back as soon as you can. Get well fast so they'll let you go. I miss you, and so does Chris."

Mom came back as she was saying goodbye. "Well, I talked them into keeping your room number a secret. It's the best I can do right now, except for staying right here beside you. Just let that monster try to get past me to hurt my daughter. He'll learn that the wrath of a mother is not something to contend with."

Miranda smiled. "I love you, Mom." She closed her eyes, suddenly too weary to hold them open.

Chapter Sixteen

Throughout the long, boring days in the hospital, Miranda hounded her father to do more to keep the horses safe. She begged him to stay in the barn with them. Mom begged him not to. "Barry, you mustn't sleep in the barn, waiting for that madman to come in and shoot you. Let the sheriff send someone."

Miranda didn't want her dad to get hurt or killed. She'd never forgive herself, but the sheriff wouldn't stake out the place with nothing more to go on than Miranda's fears.

Finally, Dad gave her some hope. "Here's what I've done. I've parked the camper close to the barn and put the baby monitor in Starlight's stall with the receiver by my bed in the camper. I've also got Little Brother with me. I'm sure he'll bark if anyone comes during the night," Dad said, referring to the big black Newfoundland cross that was the family pet. "If I hear anything suspicious, I'll call the sheriff."

"But..."

"I know. Hicks could do something before the sheriff got here. That's why I have my hunting rifle with me."

Other than hoping Hicks would be arrested before he could attack, it was the best Miranda could ask for.

She tried to think of other things throughout the day. A nurse helped her into the shower. It felt wonderful as long as the stream didn't hit her leg wound which was still bandaged and wrapped in plastic to keep it dry.

Miranda called Laurie when she knew she'd be home from school.

"You're missing so much," Laurie said. "You will be so overloaded with homework! I can help you with that, but what's worse, you're missing tryouts for the choir."

"What do you mean. I'm in choir. They aren't kicking me out, are they?"

"Of course not. I'm talking about the chamber choir. That's Flanders' small group of kids from the regular choir. He calls it the Harmonics. He's holding auditions tomorrow and choosing the best singers for special concerts and music festivals. It will be so much fun. I'll beg him to let you try out when you get back."

"It would be fun. I'm sure you'll get in. You have a beautiful voice." Miranda liked to sing and she loved doing things with Laurie.

"I sure hope so. I think it will be great to get to go on tour and have special practices and do special programs here at school, too. Mr. Flanders has really made music important in this high school."

"What if he only picks juniors and seniors? Do we have a chance as freshmen?"

"He says that won't make a difference, but we'll see. He's looking for voices that harmonize well. I think he really wants to win at the state music festival at the end of the year."

"If one of us makes it, I hope we both get in."

"Me, too, because I won't do it without you. I'll tell him that."

"Laurie, don't give up a chance like that because of me. You've got to accept if you get chosen, even if I don't."

"Really? Well, I'll think about it, but if Flanders has a heart, he'll let you in, too."

"What else is going on at school?"

"Same old stuff," Laurie said. After a pause she asked, "What is wrong with Christopher, do you know?"

"What do you mean?"

"He mopes around like his head's in the clouds. He stares out the window looking like a lost puppy. Ms. Morgan had to call on him three times before he heard her yesterday, and then he didn't have any idea what we were discussing."

"Beats me," Miranda said. Could he be thinking of her? Her whole body grew hot at the thought. She was glad Mom had left to get some lunch because she knew her face was red. "Maybe he's worried about the horses," Miranda finally thought to say. "I know I am."

"Yeah. That may be it," Laurie said, although she didn't sound convinced.

Miranda watched TV for the rest of the day, but couldn't find anything that took her mind off the horses—and Chris. She thought a lot about him after talking to Laurie. She remembered how the kiss turned her legs to jelly. Good thing she was lying down. She berated herself for feeling that way.

She shut off the TV early in the evening and fell into a fitful sleep. Even though she had no fever, her dreams were nightmarish. Hicks took on giant proportions in her dream, and she and Starlight, though they ran like the wind, could never get away from him.

When she woke the next morning, she called home first thing. "Dad, are you okay? Are the horses still there? Did he come?"

"Hold on, Mandy. I just got to the barn. Nothing happened. No one came. The horses are all fine. I think you worry too much. Aren't you supposed to be getting well so you can come home?"

"I think I'm well enough, if they'll just let me out of here."

The doctor came in about an hour later while Miranda was ordering breakfast. He examined her leg and said, "Looking good, young lady. You have no fever, the redness is gone from your leg, and the swelling is down. It's healing nicely. I see no reason why you can't go home today."

Miranda cheered and asked, "Can I go right now?"

As soon as they get you checked out. I've signed the order. You'd better go ahead and get breakfast ordered, though. Sometimes it takes a while to get through the paperwork."

He wasn't kidding. It was noon before a nurse took Miranda to the car in a wheelchair. Mom loaded all the flowers and balloons that she'd received. When they were finally on the road, she asked, "Mom, can you drive any faster?"

Chapter Seventeen

Miranda walked on crutches into the living room and stopped. "Wow, what is this? It looks like a party. Did I miss someone's birthday?"

Balloons, crepe paper streamers, and banners decorated the room. Grandma stepped out of the kitchen and hugged her. Almost immediately, three pair of arms wrapped around her, knocking one of her crutches to the floor.

"Welcome home, Mandy!' yelled Margot, Elliot, and Kort.

"Careful!" Grandma warned. "Don't squeeze her left leg. I'm sure it's still sore."

"Sorry, Miranda," Elliot said as he picked up the fallen crutch.

"No problem, Elliot. I don't really need the crutch, and you didn't hurt me. My leg's just a little sore."

"We all made presents for you," Margot said. "Sit in this chair. I decorated it just for you. "

Dad's big recliner was covered with a patchwork quilt, several pillows, and a large paper sign that stretched across the back. "Welcome Home, Miranda!"

"Thanks! Wow! I don't know what to say." Miranda limped to the chair and sat down. Elliot put a paper crown on her head. "I didn't expect anything like this." Miranda said. "I don't know what I did to deserve it, but..."

"Mom?" a loud baby voice interrupted her. "Me up."

"Coming, Kaden," Mom said, hurrying to the nursery. "I'm glad you're up. Big sister just got home."

Mom came back carrying a tousled toddler on her hip. When he saw Miranda, he leaned toward her, holding out both arms to her. Mom set him in her lap.

"Where's Dad?" Miranda asked as packages and envelopes were piled in her lap around Kaden. It was traditional that gifts were never opened until the whole family gathered around to watch.

"He's coming. I see him and Grandpa walking from the barn," Margot said.

"Does your leg hurt a lot?" Kort asked.

"Not so much anymore. It's getting better every day."

"Who shot you?" Elliot asked. "Did the bullet stick in your leg?"

"No, it went all the way through me, but thank goodness it didn't go into Starlight. The saddle stopped it. I don't know who did it. I'd like to find out. It might have been an accident, but we don't really know."

"Dad and Grandpa are here now. You can start opening presents. Mine first," Margot said.

Grandpa strode across the floor and kissed the top of her head. "Glad to see you home and alive, Mandy. You gave us quite a scare."

"We're all glad," Dad said. "I guess you'll never doubt

how much your siblings care about you. This party was all their idea."

"Mine and Elliot's mostly," Margot said.

Miranda unwrapped the small box that Margot placed in her hand. It contained a red bandana with a horse embroidered in black in one corner so that when folded in a triangle, the horse was centered.

"Wow, Margot. This is beautiful. Did you make it?"

"Yes. Grandma taught me how to embroider. It's Starlight."

"I can tell. Thank you very much. I love it!" Miranda gave her sister a hug.

When all the presents were opened, Dad said, "Mine's in the barn. Let me carry you out to see it."

He put her down just outside the stable door and pulled a key from his pocket. He unlocked the door and opened it.

"You put a lock on the door!"

"Not just this door, but all of them. No one can get in without a key, but you can open them from the inside without one."

He walked in and she followed. Starlight nickered, and she limped over to pet him. Looking around she saw that all the horses were there, each in his or her stall. Starlight was in the center of the stable, and Queen was directly across from him. Shadow, the shiny black mare that Mr. Taylor had willed to her, looked heavy with foal. Laurie's buckskin mare, Lady, and Shooting Star were across the aisle from them. There was a stall each for Margot's little grayish-white mare, Sea Foam, and Eliot's mare, Sunny. Ebony, Shadow's almost two-year old daughter, also had her own stall. A box stall at the far end housed three youngsters—yearlings or almost yearlings. There were Sea Star, son of Sea Foam, and Knight, son of Shadow, and Lady's Moonbeam, the oldest of the three. In the wide aisle between the box stall and the tack room was a twin-size bed and a bedside table with a lamp—and a baby monitor.

"Dad! Is this so I can sleep here?" Miranda caught her father in a bear hug and looked in his eyes for what she hoped was consent.

"Yes. I knew you'd never sleep if you couldn't know your horses were safe. With the monitor on, we can hear everything. Little Brother will sleep with you so that he can help sound the alarm."

"Thanks, Dad." Miranda's eyes brimmed with tears of gratitude. She'd never expected her parents to be so understanding.

"Thank your mother, too. We planned this together."

"It's probably more solid and safer than the house with the new locks, the monitor, and of course, Little Brother," Mom said.

Miranda smiled at Mom through her tears. She felt like the luckiest girl alive.

When the rest of the family left the barn, Miranda went down he aisle and talked to each horse. She saw that Dad had fed and watered them. Shooting Star had her back to Miranda when she approached her stall.

"Hey, baby. Come see me. Are you as glad to be home as I am?"

The filly didn't move, but stood with her head down.

"Star? What's wrong?" Miranda unlatched the door and went in, speaking softly as she approached, her hand on Star's hip. The horse still didn't respond.

"Are you sleeping, lazy bones? That adventure in the mountains must have worn you out. And you haven't eaten anything. The other horses' grain is all gone, but you haven't touched yours." Miranda hugged Shooting Star around the neck, and the filly pushed the side of her head and neck against Miranda's back in a return hug. "Oh, baby. You can't be sick. After all we went through to find you, you've got to be well. Do you hear me, baby? I can't stand to lose you. I love you!"

Miranda felt a sigh shake the filly's body. Shooting Star dropped her head again.

Chapter Eighteen

Miranda locked the barn and limped to the house as fast as she could. Dad was just coming out the door.

"Dad. Something's wrong with Shooting Star. How long has she been like that?"

"Like what?"

"She hasn't touched her grain, and she just stands there like she has no energy or even any will to live. Is she sick?"

"I noticed that she's been a little stand-offish when she was in the paddock with the other horses. I have been so busy getting the stable ready that I haven't paid much attention."

Dad went with Miranda to examine Shooting Star. "She doesn't seem to have a fever or anything else that I can see," he said. "I'll get an apple out of the tack room and see if I can entice her to eat that."

Miranda stayed with Star. "I know apples are your very favorite. If you don't eat that, I'm calling Dr. Talbot right now."

Dad handed Miranda an apple slice. She held it on her flat palm under Star's muzzle. The filly lipped it up and chewed it slowly. She refused the next one.

"I'll call the vet," Dad said. "You coming with me?

There was no phone in the barn, and there was no cell phone coverage on the ranch.

"No. I'll wait here with her," Miranda said, watching her father trudge to the door. He must have worked long hours to watch over her horses and make this haven secure for them.

"Thanks, Dad," she called after him.

Dr. Talbot arrived about an hour later. He examined Shooting Star thoroughly, looking at her tongue, her throat, and taking her temperature. He felt her legs for any abnormality. He listened to her belly with a stethoscope. When he stood back, shaking his head, he said, "I can't see anything wrong with her, but she is lethargic; that's for sure. I've never seen this girl this calm since she was born."

Miranda was disappointed that he couldn't just give her horse a magic pill to bring her back to her usual feisty self. Because the longtime family vet, whom she trusted implicitly, said there was nothing wrong, she decided the best thing was to wait until her fickle little filly decided to be sociable again.

Miranda went to bed early. For one, she was exhausted, and for two, she couldn't wait to tuck in and sleep with her horses. She started out with Little Brother on the bed with her, but finally had to banish him to the rug on the floor as there just wasn't room for both of them on the twin-size bed.

She breathed in the aromas she loved—horse and hay. The sounds of hooves drumming the hardwood floors and the occasional blowing, snorting, and nickering of a foal to its mama were music to her ears. She read for a while. When she dropped her book on her face, she turned off the lamp. "Goodnight, Starlight; good night, Shooting Star; good night Moonbeam; good night, Lady; good night... Sleep overtook her before she could get halfway through the list.

She didn't awaken until a voice came over the baby monitor. "You awake, Mandy? I didn't hear a thing from you or Little Brother except a little snoring, so I'm guessing there was no madman attack."

"Hi, Dad. Is it morning already? It's still dark in here."

"Time to get up and get ready for school. The bus'll be here in an hour."

"Thanks. I'll be right in."

Little Brother trotted down the aisle to the door and woofed in his low rumbly voice.

"Okay. I'll let you out, but then a little treat for the horses before I go in." She unlocked the door and left it ajar for more light as she went back to the tack room for apples. She sliced three of them in quarters and headed down the aisle, feeding a quarter to each horse.

She was a third of the way down the aisle when Little Brother began barking. Her heart skipped a beat and she dropped Ebony's apple on the floor. She wished she'd locked the door. A car door slammed and she heard Chris greet Little Brother who immediately quit barking. She breathed a sigh of relief and smiled. When she got to the door, the dog's tail was wagging wildly. "You're early. I just woke up."

"I came to help move the horses and muck out stalls," Chris said with a smile.

"Thanks. I overslept. Sorry to still be in my pajamas. Here. I started at the other end of the aisle and gave each horse a treat up to Ebony. Would you feed the rest while I get dressed. I'll be right out to help you." Dumping the apples in Chris's hands, she met his blue eyes and felt herself blush. She turned and limped to the house as fast as her game leg would allow, leaving her crutches behind.

After a very quick shower, she put on a clean pair of jeans and a sweatshirt, pulled on her boots, and went back to join Chris. He had already moved most of the horses to the pasture nearest the stable. Miranda led Starlight to his paddock. He had to be kept separate from the mares and fillies.

Dad came in as they were beginning to clean stalls.

"You don't have time to muck out the stalls now. You'll have to do it after school, or you'll miss breakfast and the bus."

"I can take Miranda to school, Mr. Stevens," Chris offered.

"Okay. Then come in and eat with us, unless you've already had breakfast," Dad offered.

"Thanks, I haven't. I'll come help clean the barn after school."

Miranda slipped into the bathroom to take a couple ibuprofen before sitting down to eat. She was beginning to feel tired already, and her left leg throbbed. How would she ever catch up on all her school work and keep up with her horse chores? She sighed. The smells from the kitchen brought a smile, though, as she sat down to a plate of sausage, biscuits and gravy, and scrambled eggs. There was nothing wrong with her appetite.

Chris smiled at her and dug in to his meal.

On the way to school she thanked him for coming to help. They had a lot to talk about. It turned out that he knew all about the locks on the stable doors. It had been his idea, and he'd helped Dad put them on.

"Did Star eat her apple?" she asked.

"Uh, no, come to think of it. She sniffed it and walked away. I fed it to Knight. That little guy sure likes apples."

"Star's acting funny. We had Doc Talbot look at her, and she's fine. Just being independent, I guess."

At school, the friends parted company, Miranda hurrying to meet Laurie for music and Chris to his AutoCAD class.

Laurie hugged her when they met. "I thought you were on crutches," she said.

"I can get along without them. My leg aches whether I use them or not. I'm really getting better every day."

"I talked to Mr. Flanders. He's going to let you try out for the chamber choir."

Before class, Mr. Flanders told Miranda to come try out right after school that day or not at all.

"Okay. I'll be here," Miranda said.

"Everyone in your places. Let's begin," he ordered before she had time to say another word to Laurie.

After the last class of the day she slipped her arm into Laurie's. "I shouldn't have agreed to audition.

There's no way I have time for this. I told Chris I'd ride home with him and help muck out stalls. We didn't have time this morning. Besides that, I'm going to have a ton of homework, and I never had time before I got hurt. I think I'll go back and tell him."

"No. Please. It won't take long. I know Chris'll wait for you, or I'll go with you and help clean stalls, but what horses were in the stable?"

"All of them." Miranda explained about the locks on the stable doors. "I'm sleeping out there. We're just not taking any chances of letting Hicks get near them."

"Do you think he's in the area?"

"Don't know, but if he's not, I think he will be. Why else would he come to Montana except to get his revenge on me?"

"Could be other reasons, but I suppose it's best to be prepared," Laurie conceded. "Tell you what, I'll go with Chris and help clean stalls."

"Okay, but I almost hope I don't get in. I don't know how I'll have time for it."

"Miranda!" a voice called from behind her. "It's about time you came back to school."

She turned to see Dennis, a good-looking classmate whom she'd gone to a party with when they were in eighth grade. It had not been a good time.

"Uh oh," Laurie said. "Be careful. Jody just broke up with him, and he's on the prowl.

Miranda ducked into the music room and closed the door. Flanders had her sing one song and told her he'd let her know his decision soon.

Chapter Nineteen

Miranda groaned when she saw Dennis talking to Laurie in the hallway the next morning. Most of the girls considered Dennis the handsomest, most charming, and coolest guy in the freshman class, if not the whole school. It was no secret that the Stephanie, Lisa, Kimberly, and Tammy were jealous of Jody Clark when Dennis began dating her last year.

Miranda avoided him as much as possible. That hadn't been so hard when Jody was hanging around—or onto—him everywhere he went. She tried to get past him without being noticed.

"Miranda, wait up!" Dennis grabbed her arm before she could dodge into the girls' restroom. "I hear you're joining the chamber choir. I'm happy about that."

"I don't know if I will. I might not even be accepted."

"Oh, you'll get in. Flanders might give the impression that he's doing you a favor by letting you audition, but don't let him fool you. If you hadn't asked him, he'd be begging you to join."

"Oh, yeah, sure," Miranda said. "I'm not that good."

"I didn't say you were. I just meant he's desperate."

"Oh, well, thanks." Miranda jerked her arm from his grasp.

"Hey, we'll have fun when we travel. I can't wait."

"I haven't said I'd join. Now, if you'll excuse me, I've got to get to class."

"Choir is our first class. I'll walk you there."

"No, you go ahead. I'll be there later." She stepped around him, grabbed Laurie by the arm, and went into the girls' room.

"Can you believe that jerk?" Miranda croaked. "Well, there's another good reason not to join the travel choir."

"Oh, no, you don't. You can't let Dennis stop you from joining," Laurie said. "And forget what he said about Flanders being desperate. It's your voice that will get you in."

"I don't think Dennis even likes me. I don't know why he's plaguing me now."

"Probably wants to make Chris jealous. He just wants what other people have."

"Well, nobody has me. And if that's the reason, why doesn't he chase you? You're far prettier, and far more taken. Anyone can see you and Bill are in love."

"You would be taken, too, if Chris had his way."

"You don't know that."

"Oh, yeah? Anybody with eyes should know that. The difference between the way Chris and Dennis look at you is limerence."

"What the heck is limerence?"

"I have it written down in my notebook. I'll show you later. Right now we'd better get to class."

Mr. Flanders smiled at Miranda as she entered the room. "Congratulations, Miranda. You've been selected to join our elite group of singers. Our first rehearsal is right after school this afternoon. We'll meet for one hour."

"Oh. I don't know if I can come. I might have to back out, Mr. Flanders. I'm sorry, I shouldn't have tried out. I..."

"Talk to me after class," he said, frowning. "Now, everyone, take your seats."

Laurie scribbled a note to Miranda. "Please!!!! Don't Back Out. PLEASE!!"

"I have stalls to clean. Chris is helping me, and I told him I'd ride home with him," Miranda scribbled back.

"I didn't think you'd be one to let limerence intrude on what you want," Laurie whispered.

Miranda rolled her eyes and shrugged her shoulders.

When class was over, Laurie told her she'd wait outside the door.

"Now, Miranda," Mr. Flanders asked, "why would you have to back out? This opportunity is only open to a few. You have a talent that I'd hate to see go to waste."

"I have a lot of chores to do every night. I can't expect someone else to take care of my horses for me."

"You'd be home by five. Isn't that early enough to start your chores?"

"It gets dark early. Sundown is earlier every day. I have to be sure I have all the horses inside before dark."

"Well, being a city boy, I can't tell you how you should run your ranch, but there must be some way you could sing with us. Truth be told, we need your voice. I only have two altos, and neither of them have as strong a voice as you do. We need someone with perfect pitch to carry them."

"I'm sorry, but I don't see any way to make it work. I should have thought of that before I tried out. Right now, it's extremely important to be home." Miranda thought of the threat of Martin Hicks and wished she didn't have to go to school at all.

"I'll tell you what. Give it a try. If you can find any way to come today, I'll change rehearsal time to lunch hour from here on out."

Miranda couldn't believe she was important enough for him to make such a change, but she was flattered. "I can call Dad and see if he could help Chris just for today, but he's awfully busy."

"Okay. Please let me know before rehearsal tonight. We're going to be singing some difficult pieces, and I want them perfected before our first concert."

When Miranda got a chance to call home just before lunch, her Mom listened to her quandary and then said. "Hold on."

Grandma came on the line. "Miranda, you stay and rehearse. I'll make sure the barn is clean and the horses are in. Margot and Elliot will do their part, of course, and, like you say, Chris is coming to help. You just don't worry. It's very important that you use your talents—all of them. It will do you good to have something in addition to your horses to focus on and develop."

Miranda thanked her grandmother, and went to find Chris. When she approached, she saw his eyes light up.

She felt her own breath catch. She had the same feeling in her stomach that she got when dropping down a big hill on a roller coaster.

He looked disappointed when she told him she wouldn't be riding home with him after all. "Grandma and maybe Dad will be taking my place tonight, but after this we'll practice at noon."

"Okay." Chris said, not quite accomplishing his obvious attempt to sound nonchalant. "I'll see you in the morning, then. I'll come earlier so we can get more done before school."

The high school choir had twenty-nine students in grades 9-12. Ideally, there would be sixteen, four each of sopranos, altos, tenors, and bass in the elite group that Mr. Flanders dubbed The Harmonics. With a shortage of boys, that was impossible. With Miranda, there were twelve. Four sopranos, three altos, four tenors, and one bass. There were four seniors, three juniors, two sophomores, and three freshmen: Laurie, Miranda, and Dennis.

Miranda thought Flanders had chosen well when she heard the voices blend during their warm-up session. When he passed out the sheet music for the first song they would learn, Miranda was a little astonished. She liked the song, but it would be challenging. She liked that the altos often alternated with the sopranos to carry the melody.

"You will notice that there are two arias—one alto and one tenor. In a few weeks, I'll be choosing singers for those parts. Find them and practice if you're interested in singing solo."

When class dismissed, Dennis caught up with her and Laurie, "Miranda, wouldn't it be cool if you and I get the solo parts?"

"Why would that be cool?"

"You know, two freshmen chosen ahead of the upperclassmen?"

"Exactly why it won't happen." Miranda took Laurie's arm and walked on. Dennis matched her steps.

"How are you getting home, Miranda?"

Miranda hadn't thought about that until this moment. Before she could think of an answer, Dennis said, "I'll drive you."

"No, thanks. Dad will come get me. He's probably waiting out front." Miranda squeezed Laurie's arm and stopped. "Now, if you'll excuse us, Dennis, Laurie and I have some things to talk over."

"Fine. I can take a hint," Dennis said, turning to walk out the front door.

"See?" Miranda said as the door closed behind him. "I shouldn't have joined. And I'm sure not going to try for the aria. If I have to put up with him bugging me every day, I'll quit."

"Calm down!" Laurie said, grinning. "He just offered you a ride, you refused, and he left. He'll get the point and leave you alone. And I think you'll get the aria whether you try for it or not."

Laurie poked a piece of paper into Miranda's music folder. "Read this when you get home. You're the best,

Miranda. I'll see you in the morning," she said as she walked on down the hall to the side door, which was closest to her house only a couple blocks away. Miranda smiled and turned toward the front entrance.

Miranda felt a warmth spread through her body when she saw Chris's little pickup parked in front of the building. The feeling disappeared quickly when she saw Dennis leaning on the driver's side window. Just as the door to the building slammed closed behind Miranda, Chris's pickup backed away. Dennis turned toward her, smiling. He walked to his bright yellow Mustang and opened the passenger's side door, gesturing toward it with a bow.

Chapter Twenty

Miranda yelled, "Chris! Wait! Stop!"

But Chris continued to back up, looking over his shoulder. He had his music cranked to high volume so there was no way he could hear her. He always turned his music up when he was mad.

She spun around to go back inside. The door wouldn't open. Locked.

She ran down the walk, waving her arms, hoping Chris would look back and see her. His taillights disappeared around a corner.

"What did you tell him?" Miranda yelled as she spun toward Dennis.

"I told him I'd take you home. No need for him to wait while you and Laurie gabbed. He seemed fine with that."

"You liar!" Miranda shoved Dennis with both hands when he reached for her. "I'm not riding anywhere with you, so forget it. And don't touch me!"

"You aren't afraid of me, are you?" Dennis asked, his eyes big and his brow furrowed. "Miranda, you're breaking my heart."

"Bull!" Miranda said as she searched her pocket for her cell phone. Not finding it, she remembered she'd left it plugged into the charger on her dresser at home.

She couldn't seem to get in the habit of carrying it. So much of the time, she was at home where there was no cell service.

"What?" Dennis asked, grinning. "No phone? Looks like you're stuck here with no way to get home but in my car. I bet you've never ridden a horse as smooth and fast as my little Mustang. He stroked the top of his car.

Miranda glared at him, hoisted her backpack onto her shoulder, and strode past him, trying not to limp.

"It's a long way to walk in the dark, Miranda. You never know who's out there, waiting for a chance to do you in."

Miranda slowed down as she thought of Hicks. Wouldn't he love finding her alone in the dark. She couldn't let Dennis see her fear, though. When she heard the Mustang's motor purr to life, she walked faster.

The yellow car idled beside her, and Dennis opened his window.

"You don't have to get in. I'll just drive along beside you to keep you safe. I heard there was a stranger in town asking about you."

Miranda looked at him, but kept walking. "Who?"

"Don't know his name. Big, stocky, dark-haired guy."

She wished she knew if Dennis were lying. But his description filled her mind with a vivid picture of Hicks as he'd looked when he had attacked her and her horse.

"Who told you that?"

"The lady at the gas station. I saw the guy talking to her and asked her who he was. She didn't get his name, but said he asked where you live."

"Did she tell him?"

"She said she didn't. He was a mean-looking dude!"

Miranda slowed down, thinking. Her leg was beginning to throb, and she sure didn't want to meet up with Hicks in the dark.

"So, what will it be, Miranda? You wanna get in or shall I idle my car all the way to your house? It's really not that good for the engine."

Miranda sighed and got in.

Dennis grinned and started showing off, taking off quickly, going through the gears, burning a little rubber with each shift. At the speed he drove, it didn't take long until they were at her driveway. He approached it too fast and skidded sideways as he turned in, stopping a few inches short of the mailbox.

Miranda waited for him to back up and try again to hit the driveway, but instead he turned off the motor and leaned toward her. "We need to talk, Miranda. I think we got off to a bad start with that thing at Tammy's party last year. I'm really sorry about that. I want you to know you've changed me. I don't smoke pot anymore—thanks to your good influence."

Miranda pounded on the door. "How the heck do I get this thing open?" She'd been struggling to find the door lock ever since he stopped.

"Chill, baby. It's locked. A child-safety thing. I control it from my side. Now, listen. I could love you. I've wanted to be with you ever since I moved here. You're different from all the other girls I've dated." He had his arm over her shoulder, pulling on her. She pulled away.

"Come on. I'm dying to hold you, kiss you, and hear you say you're mine." He unbuckled her seat belt and pulled her across the console.

"I hate you, Dennis. Now unlock the door!"

He wrapped his arms around her, pinning hers to her side.

She twisted and thrashed until her head bumped hard against his nose. He let go for an instant and she pulled on the door handle to the driver's side door. The interior light came on. She found the door unlock button. With her hand on his sternum, she shoved herself back into the passenger seat and wrenched the door open.

He grabbed her arm and cursed, calling her every nasty name she'd ever heard and then some. He squeezed her arm tighter. Twisting, she swung her other arm and punched him as hard as she could in the belly.

"Umph," he moaned, releasing her. She jumped out of the car and ran as fast as she could to the horse barn. The door was locked and she didn't have the key. She knocked, hoping that Dad was inside. Little Brother barked, but no one came to the door.

She was halfway to the house when she heard Dennis's car start. She panicked as she measured the distance to the back door. Could she get there in time? When she saw the headlights swing around as he backed away and onto the road, she breathed a sigh of relief and watched the taillights grow smaller in the direction of town.

The back door slammed. "Miranda, is that you?"

"Yeah, Dad." Miranda thought fast. She wasn't ready

to talk about what had just happened.

"You okay?" Dad asked.

"Yeah. I went to the barn first, but I don't have a key."

"Well, come on in the house. I'll walk you to the barn when you're ready. Your mom saved a plate for you, in case you haven't eaten." As they walked side by side to the house, he added, "The horses are all tucked in and fed, thanks to Chris." Dad looked around. "Did he leave already?"

"Yeah," Miranda muttered. *He left all right. Left me to the wolf!* She was as angry at Chris as she was at Dennis. Maybe even angrier.

Miranda was up early. She had showered, dressed for school, and was leading Starlight to his paddock when Chris arrived.

He was sullen and didn't speak to her as he went into the barn to get Queen. They both went about their work, moving horses and mucking stalls without saying a word to each other. Elliot and Margot came and took their horses to pasture just before bus time.

"We'll clean our stalls after school. Okay?" Elliot said as the bus rounded a corner a mile away.

"No problem, you'd better get going."

As Margot and Elliot ran to the end of the driveway to wait, Chris said. "Don't you want to catch the bus, too, Miranda? I'm sure you don't want to ride in my dumpy little truck after taking a spin in Dennis's gaudy yellow car." The sarcasm in his voice fueled Miranda's rage.

"What? Oh, don't you go there. I'd walk before I got

in your truck after you left me stranded last night. And I thought we were supposed to be friends!" Miranda threw the pitchfork into a stack of straw. The tines sank deep into a bale and the handle quivered like a tuning fork for a full minute. She felt as if every fiber in her body quivered in the same way as she stomped out of the barn.

"Hey, wait! What are you talking about? You're the one who didn't want to ride with me."

Miranda stopped and faced Chris. "How do you know what I wanted? You sure didn't wait around to ask me. No, you drove away like you couldn't get away from me fast enough. Oh, shoot! There goes the bus. I'll have to get Dad to drive me. I'm sure you couldn't stand to be with me that long."

Chris looked confused—and shocked—as if someone had just sucker-punched him.

"Miranda," he said. "You told Dennis you wanted to ride in his new car. He said you needed to talk since you were going to be singing a duet and needed to schedule practice time."

"That's what he told you?" Miranda asked. "And you believed him?"

"Well, yes, he was pretty convincing and, after all, his car is a lot nicer than my old truck."

"Dang it, Chris. If you don't know me any better than that, I don't know how you can call me a friend, let alone say you love me."

She headed for the house, calling over her shoulder. "You can go, Chris. I'm riding with Dad."

Chapter Twenty-one

Dad was replacing a light switch when she asked for a ride to school. He made her wait until he was done.

"Why didn't Chris wait for you?"

"I told him you could take me," she'd answered. "Sorry. I didn't know you were busy."

"I'm pretty much always busy. You know that."

She didn't argue but was about ready to start walking when he finally told her to get in the pickup.

Choir met every Monday, Wednesday, and Friday. Miranda volunteered as a teacher's assistant on Tuesday and Thursday. She got school credits for it. She loved working with the little kids and hated to be late.

When she walked into the first and second grade classroom, Mrs. Powell, the teacher, said, "Oh, there you are. I just called the office to see if you were sick today. I have a stack of papers for you to correct; but first, please help Anna with her workbook page."

She was almost done grading the papers when the bell rang. She hurried to finish and ran to her next class.

Laurie, who was saving a seat for her, looked up with her usual radiant smile. "Did you read the note I left for you in your music folder," she asked.

"Uh, no. I forgot about it. Things got pretty crazy after you left. I'll tell you about it at lunch."

Laurie leaned closer and whispered, "Does it have anything to do with Chris—and Dennis?"

"Yeah. How'd you know that?"

"When I got here, I saw them standing outside, arguing. It looked like Chris was about to punch Dennis, but Dennis held his hands up and walked away." Laurie looked sideways at the teacher and added, "I asked him what happened to his nose. It's got a bandage over it. He just mumbled something about a baseball breaking his nose. He sure wasn't friendly."

"Really? Oh, my gosh! I have so much to tell you."

The teacher was talking, so both girls opened their books and paid attention.

As Miranda followed Laurie through the lunch line, Chris approached her. "Miranda, we have to talk. You've got to let me explain. And if Dennis…"

"Not now, Chris. I'm eating with Laurie. Girl talk."

"I bet my ears will burn," Chris said with a sigh. "Okay. I'll wait till I see you at your place then, unless you let me give you a ride home. Please?"

"I'll ride the bus," Miranda said, determined not to forgive Chris too easily.

When Miranda sat down, she asked Laurie, "You heard of any Hicks sightings?"

"No, why? Have you?"

"Just from Dennis, and you know what a liar he is."

"Yes, I do. I think the baseball story was a lie, too. Am I right?"

"Yes, unless you call my head a baseball. Here's what happened." Miranda launched into the whole story, telling Laurie everything that happened after they parted in the hallway.

"And I don't think he'll mess with me again," she concluded.

"I hope you're right."

"Why do you say that?"

"I just mean he seems to have a way of holding a grudge and getting even. I hope I'm wrong, but you should watch your back."

"Men! What a better world this would be without them," Miranda said.

"A pretty boring one, I'd say." When Miranda didn't answer, she asked, "Do you have a date to the Snowball Dance? I'm going with Bill."

The high schoolers never missed a chance to have a party. The seniors had talked the staff into letting them host a dance to celebrate winter and, "make it snow," they said. "Sort of like a rain dance, only more fun."

"No," Miranda answered Laurie, "I don't want one. I'm staying home with my horses that night and every night until I know that Hicks is safely locked up again."

"You'll miss out on a lot of fun. I wouldn't miss the dance for anything."

"That's because you're in love. Thankfully, I don't have that problem."

"Yeah, sure you don't. "

"I don't."

"If you're through eating, let's go to the library. If you didn't read the note I put in your folder, I'll show you what it said."

Laurie led the way to the library and logged into one of the computers. She opened up a dictionary page and turned the screen toward Miranda.

"Here, read this. It's what ails you and me and every teenage girl—and boy—that I know, and apparently a lot of older people, too."

"Limerence?" Miranda asked, and then read out loud. "Limerence: an involuntary state of mind which results from a romantic attraction to another person combined with an overwhelming, obsessive need to have one's feelings reciprocated." She looked at Laurie. "Where did you come across a word like that?"

"I saw it in one of Mom's novels. I tried looking it up in our dictionary, but it wasn't in there, so I went online and found all kinds of articles about it."

"I never heard of it. But what's your point?"

"When I see how Chris looks at you, I know that he has it. Dennis, of course, does not. He's just a jerk."

"It seems to me that limerence is just another word for a crush—maybe a super crush. And I don't have it."

"Come on, Miranda. Confess. Your heart races when you see him unexpectedly, and your stomach flips when he calls. Right? You think of him when he's not around."

"Maybe I do, and maybe I have, but here's the part that I won't let happen. I won't let an overwhelming, obsessive need control my actions. I just won't." She paused, then added. "Besides, I'm mad at him right now."

"Well, I suppose that's okay. But what I worry about is that you let your need to stay in control have power over you."

"That's crazy."

"No, I don't think so. You're so determined not to fall in love, that you talk yourself into hating one of your best friends, and you treat him accordingly. He won't stick around forever." Laurie touched Miranda's arm. "Don't run him off, Miranda. He's a good guy."

When the last class let out, Miranda hurried to the parking lot. Good. Chris's truck was still there. She put her backpack in the back and waited.

"Miranda! I thought you were riding the bus." Chris grinned. "I hope this means you changed your mind."

"I did. Like you said, we need to talk."

Chris opened the passenger-side door for her and then slid into the driver's seat, but didn't put the key in the ignition. "I'm really sorry, Miranda. I've been thinking all day about what you said. I was stupid to believe Dennis. But I did, and then I was so mad—and hurt—that I guess I just turned my brain off. You were right when you said that if I really knew you, I'd have known he was lying. I would have if I'd stopped to think."

"Apology accepted. Sorry I got so mad about it. I guess I wouldn't have if I didn't really care about you. I do. I want us to be friends forever. You know that." Miranda looked sideways at him as her face heated up. It wasn't easy to admit she was wrong and even harder to tell him that she had feelings for him. And there was not doubt about it. She did.

"I want that, too, Miranda. I don't want to do anything to spoil our friendship because I care about you more than anyone in the world. That's a fact and you might as well accept it." He started the pickup.

"Sounds like limerence," Miranda said, smiling.

"What?"

"Nothing. Just a crazy new word Laurie found in the dictionary." To change the subject she added, "Now tell me, have you heard anyone say they've seen the likes of Hicks around here?"

"No, and I probably would know if they had. This is a small town, and the general store is a pretty good hub for gossip."

"Figures. One more thing Dennis lied about."

"Tell me what happened last night. Please?"

So Miranda did. There were tears in Chris's eyes when she finished just as he pulled up to the barn.

"I'm so sorry I let that happen. Will you forgive me?"

"I already have, Chris. And it sure feels good to know you and I are still friends. By the way, would you come over here instead of going to the Snowball Dance? We can sit in the barn and play cards and drink hot chocolate—have our own party."

"I'd love that. Will your parents approve?"

"I think so, as long as the baby monitor is on all evening. It won't be completely private, but we can still have fun."

Actually, it wasn't private at all. When Miranda said the word "party," three children and one toddler said, "Yea! Can we come?" So Mom made popcorn and hot chocolate, and Dad brought a TV monitor and DVD player to the barn. Margot brought her fresh-baked cookies, and she, Kort, and Elliot put on their warmest footie pajamas and brought sleeping bags and pillows. Miranda and Chris broke a bale of straw for a bed for the kids on the floor. Mom even joined them for the first half hour so that Kaden could be part of the fun. When he fell asleep, Mom said, "Goodnight. Have fun, and don't stay awake all night." She carried her sleeping bundle to the door before turning to call to Miranda. "Come lock this door behind me. And keep it locked. Oh, wait. Let Little Brother in first."

Miranda was surprised that Mom didn't say anything about Chris going home. And he didn't. She and Chris watched another movie after the other kids fell asleep. When she awoke the next morning, still in her jeans, sweatshirt, and boots and lying on the straw, she saw him curled up on her bed, sound asleep. She was covered with a blanket from the bed, and he had a thin sheet over him. Kort and Elliot were gone, and Margot lay sound asleep between her and Little Brother.

Miranda got up and put her blanket over Chris. He smiled in his sleep, and her heart did a funny tickle dance in her chest. *Limerence,* she thought. *God save me from limerence, but help me enjoy it, too.* Then she went to move Starlight to his paddock.

Chapter Twenty-two

Miranda opened the door to a blast of cold wind that flung a flurry of large snowflakes in her face.

"Whoa!" she yelped.

What a change from the past several days of blue skies, sunshine, bare ground, and temperatures in the 60s. She stepped out into four inches of powder and said to Starlight, "I guess there will be no pasture for you or the others today. I'll clean your stall and put you back inside with some hay and water."

Starlight dipped his nose into the snow and snorted. He danced sideways, letting Miranda know that he felt like playing. Laughing, she trotted alongside him to his paddock. She took off his halter and said. "Go for it, boy. Do all the bucking and playing you want while I get the barn clean."

She met Chris leading Queen on her way back to the barn. Little Brother romped along beside them, looking like a shadow in the thick-falling snow.

"Welcome to winter," Chris called to her.

"Yeah. About time, I guess," Miranda called back.

"I was in no hurry for this," Chris answered. "But I'm glad I didn't go home last night. I'll be right back to help clean stalls."

Margot was sitting up, rubbing her eyes when Miranda came back in. "Mom just called. Breakfast will be ready in twenty minutes.," she said.

"Margot your eyes are all red and swollen."

"I feel horrible. Do you think you could do my chores today?"

"You look like you feel terrible. Do you have a cold?"

"I don't know. I felt fine when I went to bed. My throat itches, my nose is stopped up, and my eyes burn. I might be allergic to the straw."

"Oh, I bet that's it. I'm sorry. You go on and let Mom doctor you. Chris and I'll get Sea Foam and the foals."

Margot let out a little screech when she opened the door. "I can barely see the house. I'm going to run for it."

Chris and Miranda worked side by side, leading horses out to the corral. They began cleaning stalls, but only had the box stall for the foals done when Mom called again. "Come in now before breakfast gets cold. You've got all day to clean stalls."

"Let us bring the foals and yearlings in. We can do the rest after we eat," Miranda said.

When they finished and headed to the house, the snow was about eight inches deep with no sign of letting up. Miranda sat on a kitchen chair, took off her boots, and massaged her half-frozen feet. "I hope my toes warm up while we eat. I'm going to wear my snow boots when we go out to finish chores. Cowboy boots are great, but not much for warmth."

"I didn't bring my warm boots," Chris said, "but we'd better get them in soon. It's not getting any nicer."

"The horses will be fine. They have the loafing shed," Dad said. "They've weathered storms like this before."

"All but Starlight. He doesn't have any shelter in his paddock except that one tree, and there are no leaves left on it."

"He's a hearty, healthy, Montana horse." Dad said. "This is the first winter he's been stabled every day. I'm sure he'll be fine. Eat your breakfast and then do your homework while you warm up."

The phone rang. Margot ran to answer it and then carried the phone to Chris. "It's your mother. She doesn't sound very happy."

"Hi, Mom." Miranda watched Chris's face and knew he was getting a royal chewing out.

"Mom, I'm sorry. I thought you knew I was staying over. You want me to come home now?"

He paused and held the phone away from his ears. Miranda could hear Mrs. Bergman's voice, but couldn't make out the words.

Chris put the phone back to his ear and said, "Okay, Mom. I'll wait until the roads are plowed."

When he handed the phone back to Margot, he said, "I should have called last night, but I fell asleep before the movie was over. She didn't notice I wasn't home until just now, so she can't really say she stayed up all night worrying."

"She wants you to come home?"

"There's a storm advisory saying no one should get on the road unless it's an emergency. Thankfully, she didn't think my getting home was an emergency."

"Good. I'm going to sit by the fireplace to do my homework. My toes are still numb," Miranda said as she carried her plate to the sink, rinsed it, and put it in the dishwasher. "Thanks, Mom. Breakfast was delicious."

"I think I'll have one more biscuit," Chris said. Then I'll get my homework done, too."

"I still think I should be getting the horses in. It's cold out there." Miranda looked out the window and saw nothing but a flurry of white flakes.

"Like your dad said. The horses will be all right." Mom said. "You can get some of your homework done while you warm up. We've been pretty lenient with you, but remember you're still grounded."

"Just from riding horses, right?"

"There's something in there about bringing your grades up. Do your homework."

Chris put his dishes in the dishwasher and offered to help Miranda's mom with the dishes.

"Thanks, Chris, but I've got this. If you have homework, this is the time to get started."

"Okay, thanks. My books are in my truck," Chris said, pulling on his coat.

Miranda was happy to open her books and begin writing the essay for English. She'd made notes and had an outline in her head. She really didn't feel like carrying manure out to the pile by the back door of the barn in this weather. Mucking stalls and corrals was a part of everyday life of a horse owner, but sometimes she got tired of it. So she accepted her Dad's assurance that the horses would be all right for a while. It eased her conscience and allowed her to get into her school work. She'd chosen to write about the Crow Fair and the many horse events, beautiful horses, and the skilled riders that took part in the races and rodeo.

Her conscience began to nag at her as she heard the wind banging things around outside. Her horses hadn't even been fed yet. Looking up she searched the room for Chris—and didn't find him.

"Where's Chris?" she asked, getting up from her comfortable chair by the fire.

"Isn't he in there with you?" Mom asked from the kitchen. "Did he ever come back with his books?"

"Oh, my gosh," Miranda exclaimed, peering out the window. "It's a whiteout!" She pulled on her parka and snow boots. "I've got to find him."

"Miranda, wait," Mom said. "Don't go out there without a way to find your way back. Let me get you some rope. And take the cowbell."

Miranda's heart raced as she put on her hat and gloves while waiting for Mom.

"Here. Take this clothesline rope. I'll tie the end to the door knob." Miranda stepped into the wind-driven snow and took down the cowbell that hung on a nail on the back door. Mom had put it there for decoration, but sometimes used it to call her family for a meal. Miranda set off ringing the bell and yelling Chris's name as she unwound the rope behind her.

"Christopher! Chris, where are you?" she yelled at intervals and then stopped to listen. There was only the howling of the wind and banging of things buffeted by the it. Just as she reached the end of the rope, she saw a shape in front of her. She'd come to Chris's pickup. She pounded on the hood, not willing to let go of the rope to get to where she could open the door.

"Hello?" came a voice in the wind, along with the creak of a door opening. "Miranda?"

"Chris. Here. In front of your truck."

"Dang, Miranda. It took you long enough. I thought I'd freeze to death."

"Sorry, but why were you sitting in your truck?"

"I'll tell you when we get inside, if we can get back to the house. I don't want to get lost again."

"I have a rope. It's tied to the back door." She guided Chris's hand to the rope. "Reel it in and it'll take us to the house. I'll hold onto you."

Once inside the house, Chris kicked off his boots and headed for the fireplace. "I don't think my feet will ever thaw out."

"What happened?

"By the time I got my backpack out of my truck, I couldn't see the house anymore. I couldn't see a thing but blowing snow." Chris shivered. Miranda wrapped a blanket around his shoulders.

"So you stayed in the truck?"

"No. That would have been the smart thing. I was sure I could find the house, but somehow I missed it. I must have walked right past it. When I realized I'd gone too far, I came back and missed it again. I just kept walking big circles, or at least I think that's what I was doing. I thought for sure I'd run into the house eventually. I finally ran into my truck, so I got back in and waited."

"Oh, I'm so sorry. I should have looked for you sooner. I just got so wrapped up..." Miranda's voice caught in her throat as she thought of what could have happened to him. "I'm so, so sorry."

"I thought I heard the bell and was about to get out, when you pounded on the hood of the truck. I was—am—so cold, but I was afraid to start the truck and run the heater. The snow is up to the bumper, and I thought the exhaust pipe might be plugged up."

"You did the right thing, son," Miranda's dad said. He'd just come upstairs from his workshop to hear Chris's story. "None of us realized you were in danger. I went to work in the basement just as you were going outside."

"My horses are still out in it, and they haven't even been fed yet," Miranda said.

"You're not going out in this blizzard, Miranda. After Chris's close call, I think you understand."

Mom brought Chris a cup of hot cocoa. "Are you okay?" she asked.

"Yeah, I'm cold, but alive and so thankful to be back inside a warm house. Thanks for the hot chocolate. You make the best."

Miranda went back to her homework, but couldn't concentrate on last summer's activities. She started a new essay. At the top of the page she wrote, "Don't lose your best friend in a snowstorm." *Or anywhere else, for that matter,* she told herself.

By noon, snow piled against the windows like plaster and the wind continued to howl.

"Barry, it's worse than ever out there. Please wait."

Miranda looked up to see Dad putting on his coat when she heard Mom's protest.

"I found another coil of nylon rope in the basement. We'll tie that to the end of your clothesline rope and I'll have plenty to make it to Starlight's paddock. I just want to let him in with the others and throw them a little hay. It won't take long."

"Oh, please be careful. Make sure the two ropes are tied well so they can't come apart."

"You're talking to a navy man, sugar. I know how to do a great sheep shank that won't have a chance of slipping. Don't worry." He gave Mom an affectionate kiss on the cheek.

"Okay. But hurry. I'm holding my breath until you get back." Miranda knew Mom was kidding, of course, but she also knew she was very worried. If a person got lost in this stuff, they could freeze to death before finding their way back.

When the storm hadn't let up by bedtime, Chris called his mom. She agreed that he'd have to stay overnight, having heard on the news that all the roads in the area were closed.

Miranda woke once in the middle of the night, listening to try to determine what had awakened her. Slowly she realized it wasn't a noise but the absence of it that had changed. She rose to look out her bedroom window, but it was blocked with snow. She pulled a robe over her pajamas and tiptoed through the living room. She opened the door and looked at a brilliant silver world as light from the moon glistened off endless drifts of snow. She smiled and walked back through the living room. A ray of moonlight illuminated Chris's face where he slept on the couch. *He looks as sweet and innocent as an angel,* she thought and fought the urge to kiss him. Back in her room she slipped into a dream where he kissed her and she kissed back.

Sunshine fell across Miranda's face, and Margot called to her from the doorway. "Miranda, the sun's up and it's not snowing at all."

"Oh, good. Is Chris up?"

"Everyone's up but you and Kaden. Elliot and Dad and Chris went out to start cleaning the barn."

"Why didn't someone wake me sooner?" Miranda asked, scrambling out of bed and searching for her jeans. She dressed in record time, put on her snow boots, parka, and gloves and rushed out the door.

Sunlight glared off the snow. Miranda squinted at the drifts curling around buildings and vehicles. The snow was piled high in places and the ground swept almost clean in others.

With everyone working, the barn was clean, new straw scattered on the floors of each stall, and hay and grain placed in each feeder by the time Mom called them for breakfast.

"You go ahead, Dad. We'll get the horses in so they can eat the same time we do," Miranda said. Dad agreed and headed for the house.

Miranda ran to get Starlight first while Chris led Queen to the barn. They raced each other back to the corral and met Elliot leading Sunny.

"I'll get Sea Foam for Margot," he called.

"There's Lady, waiting by the gate," Chris said.

"And here come Shadow and Ebony," Miranda said. I'll get Ebony, and then we can come back for Shadow and Shooting Star, and we'll be done."

Ebony stuck her nose in the halter, apparently eager to get to the barn and have breakfast.

Chris got back to the corral first, walked by as Miranda stopped to put the halter on Shadow. He disappeared into the shed. He came out just as Miranda was opening the gate to take Shadow through.

"Miranda, Shooting Star isn't here!"

Chapter Twenty-three

"Gone again?" Miranda had to see for herself. Shooting Star could blend in with the dark shadows of the loafing shed, couldn't she? Not as easily as the black horses, of course, but... She ran into the shed and peered into each corner. Still not convinced she walked along the entire perimeter next to the wall. No horse.

"The little devil! How did she get out, and why? Do you think Hicks got to her during the storm?"

"No, I don't. I think she escaped on her own just like she always does. Look. I think she went under the fence. Those could be tracks that the wind filled in," he said, pointing at depressions on the other side of the fence. "As for why, I can't answer that. Just because she can, I guess."

Miranda noticed that the snow at the spot Chris indicated was a little lower on both sides of the fence, but covered still with fresh powder. She sighed. "I think you're right. She must be somewhere in the big pasture. She could be down by the river or clear up on Silver Butte—or over it. We've got to find her."

"It won't be easy tracking her in all this snow. The indentations disappear in that drift by the big juniper."

"You're right. The sooner we go the better chance we'll have, though," Miranda said. "I'll put Shadow away, and then let's saddle up,"

"Let's eat first. We'll need a good breakfast in our bellies before we tackle those snow drifts. And the horses need time to eat," Chris suggested.

"Yeah, you're right. Go ahead if you want. I'll put Shadow in her stall."

"I'll walk with you," Chris said, but stopped as he heard a vehicle's engine revving.

"Look. That's Bill's jeep. Looks like he's having fun," Chris said as he changed course, climbed the corral fence, and went to meet their visitors.

Miranda quickly put Shadow in her stall and went out the front door just as the Jeep came to a stop and Laurie stepped out. She was bundled in winter clothes.

"Wow, I'm surprised you made it." Miranda said. "I'm impressed and very glad to see you."

Chris was talking with Bill about the prowess of Bill's CJ-5 Jeep, a four-wheel-drive wonder that he'd just put studded winter tires on.

"I'm glad we made it," Laurie said. "The road was plowed to the corner. We almost got stuck in a drift between there and your driveway."

"But your driveway and barnyard were the most challenging," Bill added. "And the most fun."

"We were just going in for breakfast and then we're going to go search for Star. She's run away—again!"

"Oh, that little imp!" Laurie exclaimed. "She chose a great time to escape! How long has she been gone?"

"I don't know. You'd think she'd want to stay in the shelter with the other horses, but, no. She takes off for the snowy wilds. And who knows how long she's been gone? It could have been anytime yesterday or last night."

"Bill and I can help you search, right Bill?" Laurie asked.

"Sure. And we'll join you for breakfast if you don't mind. I rousted Laurie out before her parents were up."

"Good. I'm sure there's plenty. If not, you know Mom will make more."

As the four of them ate, Miranda explained the situation to her parents. "We've got to find her. And the only way is on horseback. Please let me ride. We've got to find Star."

Mom looked at Dad with question in her eyes.

"Well," he said, "you told me you looked up her grades on the parent portal from the school's website. She has an A in every subject, right?"

Mom nodded.

"Then, I think she's learned her lesson, and this is something of an emergency."

When breakfast was over, the four teens bundled into winter clothes and headed for the barn. Miranda could hardly wait to get on her horse again.

"Do you have a horse for me?" Bill asked.

"Umm, Elliot would probably let you ride Sunny. Or else there's Ebony, but she's barely started. I haven't been able to ride her for weeks. It wouldn't be good to take Shadow out in this, pregnant as she is."

"I like a horse with a little spunk. Don't worry, I'm an expert horseman," Bill bragged.

"He is. He grew up on horses, plus he just completed a Buck Brannaman clinic this fall," Laurie said with a great measure of pride in her voice.

Limerence, Miranda thought, shaking her head.

"Okay. It will do Ebony good. I'm sure Dad will let you use his saddle."

"I'll be right back," Bill said, running to his Jeep.

He came back carrying a rifle in a scabbard. He deftly saddled and bridled Ebony and tied the scabbard to the saddle.

"You planning on poaching a deer or something?" Chris asked.

"No, but it never hurts to be prepared. Ranchers have been reporting wolf and lion kills in the hills around here."

"Speaking of being prepared," Mom called from the front door of the stable. "Margot and I fixed lunches and water for all of you. We put it in your saddle bags, Miranda. Tie it on to the back of your saddle."

"Thanks, Mom. You're the greatest."

"Be back before dark, or you won't think I'm so wonderful," Mom warned. "I mean it, Miranda. Whether you've found her or not, start back in time to get here no later than sundown. I may ground you for a year if you worry me."

Miranda mounted Starlight, Chris rode Queen, and Laurie rode Lady. They took turns breaking trail and went single file. The horses had to lunge through the bigger drifts, so it was easier on the animals to keep them on the broken trail. Starlight did most of the leading, because he was the tallest, strongest horse.

Miranda was able to see some hoof prints on the trail along the river in the spotty protection of the trees. They'd disappear in a drift but show up again farther on. Miranda stopped where the trail to Silver Butte forked to the right and another followed the river's edge. "Now, which way did you go, little girl?"

"How about Bill and I take one trail, and you and Laurie the other. Whoever sees her tracks will holler at the others, and we'll join up," Chris suggested.

"Okay. Sound good to you, Bill?" Miranda asked, twisting in her saddle to look back at him.

"Okay by me. This is a sweet horse, Miranda. If you ever want to sell her..."

"You couldn't afford her," Miranda said. "But I'll let you ride her any time you want."

Miranda chose the high road and set out on the trail to Silver Butte. Laurie urged Lady up beside her. "Good choice, Miranda. Here we don't have snow falling off the trees down our necks every few yards."

"Yeah, but it's harder to find tracks. The snow's deep out here."

"There are some kind of a tracks up in those trees," Laurie said about ten minutes later. Miranda saw them off to the left just coming out of a thicket of junipers. They hurried for a close look.

"I'd say those are wolf tracks. Pretty fresh, too." Miranda said.

"Do you think Shooting Star's up here?"

"Let's follow the wolf tracks," Miranda answered.

At the other side of the clearing, Miranda saw snow-filled prints that were big enough to be those of a horse. She followed them farther into the trees and they became clearer where the snow wasn't drifted.

"Definitely Star's tracks," Miranda said. "I hope we can make the boys hear us.

"I think so if I yell, and you whistle."

The girls turned their horses back into the clearing. Laurie began shouting. Miranda removed her gloves, put the index finger from each hand against her tongue, and forced out a whistle that could be heard for miles. They kept it up for a couple of minutes and then paused. A similar whistle came from below, and soon two horses emerged through the trees.

"We were on our way. The snow was shallow enough that we figured she couldn't have gone that way without making tracks, so we turned around," Bill said as they rode up to where the girls were.

"Besides, I'm starving. It's one o'clock," Chris said. And this clearing is the perfect place to eat. How about wiping the snow off that big rock over there?"

"I don't know. There are wolf tracks on top of Shooting Star's."

"Are her tracks much older than theirs?" Bill asked.

Miranda shrugged. "The wolf prints were made since it stopped snowing. Hers were made before that."

"Then we probably have time to eat."

"Tell you what. I'll pass out sandwiches and we can

eat while we ride. We don't have much time left, and I sure don't want to be grounded again."

"Good idea," Laurie said. "I'm a bit worried about those wolf tracks. Looks to me like there were several."

They followed the tracks through the trees for another half hour until Starlight let out a whinny that nearly shook Miranda out of the saddle. The answering neigh sounded frantic.

Miranda urged Starlight into a canter as she leaned low over the saddle to keep from konking her head on tree branches. Just past a pine thicket, she saw Shooting Star, backed up against a rock the size of a house. A pack of five wolves surrounded her.

"Hi Yah!" Miranda yelled as she urged Starlight faster into the midst of the pack. The wolves scattered.

Miranda jumped from her horse and walked to Star. The filly trembled, but stood, waiting. "Oh, you poor baby. You're bleeding. What did they do to you?" She examined Star's chest and right foreleg where blood oozed and dripped to the ground.

"Miranda, watch out!" Chris shouted. He charged toward the wolves, but they barely retreated, showing bared teeth as Queen neared. He stopped and yelled at them, but they stood their ground.

"Get back on your horse, Miranda!" Bill yelled. "Chris, get back. I'm going to shoot over their heads to scare them off."

Miranda turned and backed up against Star's chest. A very large wolf was creeping toward her. A shot rang out. The wolf stopped and sprang back. The whole pack ran into the trees. When she heard Bill shout some swear words she looked his way. He was getting up from the ground brushing snow from his gun.

"Where's Ebony?"

"Dang. I should have got off first. She jumped right out from under me and ran down the hill."

"Bill? They're coming back," Laurie said.

"Hold your horses, everyone." Bill fired again, kicking up snow in front of the wolves. They all ran back into the trees. Bill reloaded and shot again.

Star hunched between Miranda and the rock trembling. Miranda put a halter on her and led her to where Chris was holding Starlight's reins. "He was about to follow Ebony," Chris said, "but when I said, 'whoa, boy,' he stopped. You've trained him well, Miranda."

"Thanks, Chris. Let's get these horses home." She got on Starlight as Bill climbed on behind Laurie.

Miranda led the way with Star limping behind, and Chris and Queen right behind her. "I'll watch our rear," Bill said as Lady followed Queen.

About halfway down the hill, Chris yelled. "Bill, up here. They've circled around us."

Miranda gasped as two big wolves dashed across the clearing straight toward Shooting Star.

She heard a shot and the lead wolf fell just as it lunged at the bleeding filly. The other wolves faltered and then came on. Another shot, and another wolf lay dead in the snow. Three more turned back and disappeared in the trees. Miranda couldn't stop shaking and tears clouded her vision. She'd been scared half to death, and now two beautiful animals lay lifeless on blood-reddened snow. She looked back at Bill.

"I didn't want to kill them," he said. "I may be in big trouble, but they were..."

"I know, Bill. You may have just saved my life. Star's for sure. Thanks." A sob caught in her throat and she headed down the trail as Bill remounted.

They reached the fork in the trail just as the sun disappeared over the western hills. Miranda sighed. There was no way to get back by dark. She hoped Mom would understand. They were almost home when she saw something moving in the dark ahead of her. At first, she feared it was another wolf. Then she heard her father's voice.

"Miranda?"

"Dad!" As she drew closer she saw that he was riding a black horse. "You found Ebony!"

"She came home and found me. I was pretty worried about the empty saddle. Is anyone hurt?"

"Just Shooting Star. The wolves were attacking her."

"Thank God that none of you kids are hurt. You better get to the house and report to your mom as soon as we get back, Miranda. I'll put your horses up for you. You can come back and help once you get your mother calmed down," Dad said. "But that could take a while."

Chapter Twenty-four

Margot shook Miranda's shoulder and yelled, "Miranda! Wake up. Get up, Miranda. You'll be late for school. No one's done any chores yet."

Miranda groaned. Could it be Monday morning already? She felt like she could sleep a dozen more hours. "What time is it?"

"It's almost seven. I tried to wake you an hour ago by calling over the monitor, so don't be mad at me for not having any time with your horses," Margot said.

"Oh, shoot. I don't have time to go to school today." Miranda threw back the covers and noticed she was wearing her clothes from yesterday. "I've got to call Dr. Talbot and take care of Star."

It had taken her a long time to go to sleep after all the excitement. Mom required a lengthy explanation about why she was late and finally gave her a hug instead of further punishment. Her friends had gone home before she got back to the barn. She'd argued with her dad about calling Doc Talbot. Dad thought it could wait until morning, but let her call. The vet was out of town for a weekend conference. He'd be back sometime today.

"You go to school. Doc will get your message when he gets back. I'm sure he'll come right over, and I'll be here," Dad said when Miranda asked permission to skip school. "You'd better hurry. I'll finish your chores."

In choir that morning, Mr. Flanders announced that they'd leave for their first choir tour Friday morning. They would be traveling to some towns in eastern Montana and would be back Sunday night. The school Christmas program was the next Wednesday, and school let out for Christmas vacation at noon Friday. "We'll have noon practices every day this week," Mr. Flanders added. "Be there if you want to go on the tour with us. No excuses."

Miranda called home at noon. Dr. Talbot had called to say he'd been delayed. He'd be there in about an hour.

"May I come home? I have choir practice, but if I leave as soon as it's over, I'll be there by the time he is."

"Miranda, I told you I can take care of it. I'll let you know what he says when you get home."

Miranda heaved a sigh. "Okay. Gotta go. Flanders is ready to start."

Chris was waiting for her at the front door when the bell rang. On the ride home, she asked him if he could come stay in the stable with the horses while she was gone Friday and Saturday nights.

"You think Hicks is still a threat?"

"He hasn't been captured yet."

"I wonder what he's doing."

"Waiting for us to let down our guard, I'd guess. But I'm not going to."

When Miranda and Chris pulled into the yard, Dr. Talbot's truck was still parked in front of the barn.

"I thought he'd be long gone. Star must be worse than we thought." She ran to the barn and opened the door in time to collide with the veterinarian.

"Oh. Hi, Miranda," he said, grabbing her by the shoulders to keep her from falling. "Sorry. I almost knocked you down."

"No, my fault. What about Star? How bad is she?"

"Her wounds are not deep. They'll heal up nicely. I'm a bit concerned about her weight loss, though. I took a blood sample for some tests, wormed her, and ordered a supplement. Has she been off her feed ever since I last saw her?"

Miranda thought."Well, she seemed to pick up a little, but she leaves some of her hay everyday, so I've been giving her a little sweet feed. She doesn't always clean that up, either."

"Get her some high-calorie feed and add a cup of this supplement to it twice a day. I'll call as soon as I have the test results, but I can't see anything wrong with her other than she's just not eating."

Miranda and Laurie sat together on the bus as it pulled out of the school parking lot at seven Friday morning. Chris had promised to help Miranda's dad with the chores and to spend the night in the tack room until the choir got back. He'd give special care to Shooting Star.

"Don't you wish Bill and Chris were in choir?" Laurie asked as she looked around at the couples sitting together. Dennis sat beside Andrea, a sophomore.

"No, I don't. Who would take care of our horses if

it weren't for Chris? Dad and Mom wouldn't stay in the barn at night. I think they think I'm a little paranoid to worry about Hicks as much as I do."

"If Martin Hicks plans to do you any harm he sure is taking his sweet time," Laurie said.

"I know. Maybe he's not a threat—or maybe he's just waiting for me to let down my guard." Miranda shook her head. "It makes me nervous."

"Don't look now," Laurie whispered, "but Dennis keeps staring at you."

"You're imagining things. He's with Andrea," Miranda whispered back.

"Okay, look. See for yourself."

Miranda looked over her shoulder at where Dennis sat with his arm around Andrea. His eyes were on Miranda, and he winked.

Miranda jerked back to face the front of the bus. Her face burned with anger.

"See?" Laurie asked.

"What a player. I'd like to slap him."

"Poor Andrea."

"Yeah. Poor anybody who gets mixed up with him. You can bet it won't be me ever again."

"Now, don't you wish Chris had come along?"

"No, but I wish Dennis would go back where he came from." Miranda stopped herself. "Come on, Laurie. Let's talk about something pleasant. Let's promise we won't say the creep's name or mention anything about him again on this whole trip."

"It's a deal," Laurie said. "So let's talk about Bill. Did

you know he's been having nightmares about wolves?"

"Really?"

"He wouldn't admit it for a while, but I could tell something was wrong."

"He dreams about wolves chasing him?"

"No. He dreams about them crawling to him and asking him why he hurt them," Laurie said. "And in his dreams, they have big blue eyes full of tears and blood pouring out of their noses."

"Good grief! Does he feel guilty about killing them?"

"He's worried that he's going to get in trouble for it."

"Why should he get in trouble? It was me or the wolves. Besides, how do the authorities know who killed them?"

"Bill called them, of course. It was the first thing he did the next day," Laurie said. "That's one of the things I love about him. He's so honest and responsible."

"So why would he get in trouble?"

"They are pretty disappointed because one of the wolves had a radio collar. There're not many collared wolves left."

"So? It was going to kill my horse."

"I know, but it might make them prone to ask more questions than they would otherwise."

"They've been asking questions?"

"They asked Bill to come in this week and talk to them and 'answer some questions.'"

Just as Miranda was about to comment, she felt a sharp sting just beneath her ear.

"Ow! What was that?'She reached up to rub the spot and found a rubber band on her collar. She turned to see Dennis looking straight at her.

He winked again .

Miranda fought to stay in her seat when she just wanted to jump up and sock him in the nose. *I won't give him the satisfaction,* she thought. She handed the rubber band to Laurie and rolled her eyes.

Laurie looked at her questioningly and then looked back at Dennis and shook her head. "What a jerk!" she muttered.

The people of Miles City gave them a heart-warming welcome. When the concert was over, dozens of people came up to Miranda and shook her hand, telling her what a wonderful voice she had. Miranda loved to sing, and the compliments were rewarding. She and the rest of the choir found the same reception in Terry and in Glendive. People begged them to come again next year. When it was time to head home after their concert, it had begun to snow and the wind was blowing.

They were housed in the homes of community members. Laurie, Miranda, and two of the other girls were invited to spend the night in the basement rec room of a large ranch house. Tired from travel and two late nights, they didn't talk much before falling asleep.

Miranda was surprised to wake up with light coming through the windows. The plan had been to be on the road before daylight. They were to sing in a church in Billings on their way home. Miranda dressed quickly and went to the kitchen where Mrs. Buck, their hostess, was cooking breakfast. All three of the other girls were still sleeping.

"Why didn't someone wake us?" Miranda asked. "Did we miss the bus?"

"Look out the window, and I think you'll see."

Miranda walked to the big picture window in the dining room and saw nothing but white. Snow swirled around the patio where a drift on one side of the picnic table was four feet deep and the ground was swept almost bare on the other side.

"Mr. Flanders called and said the roads are closed. You can't leave until they are cleared," Mrs. Buck said. "I figured you might as well get all the sleep you need."

"Thanks," Miranda said. "It looks like you're cooking for an army. May I help?"

"I am. The rest of the choir, Mr. Flanders, and the bus driver will be here in an hour for breakfast. But I think I have everything under control. If you want to shower and then wake the other girls, go right ahead. I think you'll find everything you need in the downstairs bathroom."

Miranda thanked her, woke the other girls, and took a quick shower, mindful of saving hot water for her schoolmates. When she finished she went back to see what more she could do. The rest of the choir had arrived and were sitting in the living room watching the news on TV. A winter-weather advisory was on, warning that no one travel unless it was an emergency.

After breakfast and chores all of the choir members

were sent downstairs to the rec room to entertain themselves. The quiet room where the four girls had spent a peaceful night was suddenly loud and stuffy as kids jostled each other, yelled, sang, laughed, and turned up the TV as someone with a remote scrolled through countless channels.

"Hey, quiet, everyone." Dennis stood in the center of the room, holding a shampoo bottle. "Look what I found. I think we need to play a quiet game before the grownups come down to yell at us. I propose spin the bottle. Who's in?"

"What fun is that when there are way more girls than boys?" Brianna, a senior soprano, asked.

"Great fun for us gentlemen of the choir," Dennis said, laughing. "Two for each of us. We can handle it, can't we, guys?" He reached for Andrea's hand to pull her to her feet.

She slapped his hand away. "You're not handling me, Dennis. I don't know about anyone else, but I'm not going to play your stupid kind of games." The angry voice coming from Andrea seemed to surprise everyone. There were tears in Andrea's eyes. Her face turned bright red as everyone got very quiet and stared at her. She went into the bathroom and slammed the door.

"Way to go, Dennis," Mark, a senior and the only bass in the chamber choir, said scornfully. "You sure know how to treat a girl."

"You poor, deprived rednecks have no sense of adventure. Sometimes I wonder how I survive in this backwoods state," Dennis said. He made his way to the bathroom door where he stood waiting. "Don't worry, Mark. I'll make up with Andrea. I'm afraid I, a lowly freshman, know more about women than you do, high and mighty as you think you are."

Miranda looked at Laurie who was so engrossed in a book, she didn't seem to notice what was going on. But Miranda knew her well enough to realize that she knew exactly what was going on, but chose to ignore it.

Miranda nudged her. "I'm going outside. I think I'm getting claustrophobic."

Laurie nodded, but kept reading.

The storm had let up, but snow was still coming down lightly. Visibility had cleared, and Miranda made her way to the barn, hoping to see some of the rancher's horses. The barn was an old hip roof design with a large hayloft. The horse stalls were empty, the edges of the mangers rubbed smooth with years of horses leaning on them to get the last piece of hay from the bottom. There was a faint odor of horse sweat and manure, but the stalls were all clean. Harnesses, bridles and halters hung from hooks on the wall behind the stalls. She climbed the ladder to the loft where the fragrance of dry hay became stronger. She was surprised to see it filled with hay bales in two stacks with a space in the middle. Most ranchers chose to put their hay bales on the ground where it was easy to stack them with machines.

She climbed the stair steps of bales to her left and grasped the thick rope that was hanging from a sliding pulley—just like the one in the old barn at Shady Hills. She tested the rope and then pushed herself off the top of the haystack to glide the length of the barn. She sighed, wishing she were ten again and had nothing to deal with but her horses. Well, maybe not ten. She didn't own a horse then, but not a high schooler, traveling with total jerks.

She pushed off from the other end of the barn and glided with her eyes closed in the joy of solitude when something grabbed her foot. She looked down as she was brought to a halt. Dennis.

Chapter Twenty-five

Overcome with anger, Miranda tried to kick her foot free. His grip tightened. She wanted to hurt him. How dare he invade the only solitude she'd been able to find since leaving home for this stupid tour? No, she corrected herself, the tour, the music, and the joy of performing weren't stupid. Dennis and everything about him was.

"Let go of my foot."

Looking up with a grin on his face, Dennis taunted, "What's the matter? Aren't you glad to see me?"

"What are you doing here?"

"Looking for you. Not that it was hard to find you. Just followed your tracks through the snow."

"I wasn't hiding, but I guess I should have been. I just want peace and quiet. That excludes you."

"Hey, I like the idea of solitude. You couldn't have picked a better spot for us to be alone."

"Get out, Dennis. Leave!"

"You surely don't mean that."

"You thick-headed, egotistical scum. You should know I mean it. I don't like you. I don't want to be around you. Can I make that any more clear?"

"Not when you lead me out to a romantic hideaway

after I suggested a kissing game. It's obvious, Miranda. You wanted me all to yourself."

"I can't believe you! How can anyone be that self-centered?"

"Aw, come on, Miranda. How can I convince you that I'm serious? My intentions are honorable. You think I'm a player. Well, if I date other girls, it's just because I can't have the one I want. If you'd be my girl, I'd never look at another one. I promise."

"Get lost, Dennis. And let go of my foot."

He tightened his grip some more. She lifted her other foot and stomped down hard on his fingers.

"Ow. Damn you. Look what you've done." He held up a bloody knuckle where her boot had peeled back a layer of skin. "I swear you'll be sorry, Miranda."

"I am sorry. Sorry I ever met you. I wish you'd go back where you came from."

"I would if I could, trust me."

Dennis disappeared down the ladder, leaving Miranda hanging with nothing in reach to shove off of in order to get the rope moving again. She slowly lowered herself down the rope, trying not to let it slide too fast and burn her hands. She dropped the last three feet and climbed down the ladder. She was about to go out the door when the strong odor of cigarette smoke stopped her. She saw smoke rising above one of the stall dividers.

She hurried to investigate. Just as she thought, it was Dennis leaning back on the manger, puffing away.

"You idiot! Smoking in the barn? You want to burn it down?"

"You worry too much. How is this going to catch the barn on fire?" He flicked the cigarette, watched the ashes fall, and then crunched them with his foot.

I can't believe you're smoking. You want to sing, and yet you torture your vocal cords. Don't you know tobacco kills people?"

"Aw, sweetheart. You do care about me after all. That is so sweet."

"Don't mock me!"

"I'm not. Really. I'll quit smoking if you'll just admit you care about me and let me be your friend." He wiggled his eyebrows and winked on the word "friend."

"You have no idea what it means to be a friend to anyone. You've made yourself my enemy, and I don't care what you do to yourself. Smoke all you want. I just wish you'd stop taking advantage of Andrea and every other girl you decide to exploit."

"Exploit? I'm not exploiting anyone. I give the ladies what they want."

"And what's that?"

"Me. A charming, caring, handsome, rich kid. What's not to love?"

Miranda shook her head in disgust and turned to leave. Dennis lunged forward and grabbed her arm.

"You're such a fool, Miranda. I could give you anything you ever wanted if you didn't think you were so much better than me."

"I am better than you. And I have everything I want—except you out of my life. Now let go of me ,or I'm going to scream."

"Like anyone would hear you." He laughed, but his face was red with anger. He squeezed her arm hard and then wrenched it as he shoved her backward into a post.

Her head hit a big spike nail where a halter hung. She resisted the urge to cry out or to reach up to touch the painful spot on the back of her head. "Let go of me, Dennis, or I really will scream."

They both heard a door slam. He stepped back.

"Look, I don't mean to hurt you," he whispered. "I'm sorry if I did. I just wish you'd believe me. I really do love you. You're the only girl in the school I care about."

"Really? Then I'd hate to see how you treat the ones you don't care about." Miranda started to leave, but looked back at Dennis one more time. "You'd better put that fire out before you leave."

"What?" Dennis looked down at his feet where a few sprigs of hay were smoldering.

Miranda didn't wait to see him stomp them out.

It was past noon before the roads were cleared and the bus dug out so they could travel. They stopped at a McDonald's in Bozeman for a late supper, and didn't get back to the school until 10:15 p.m. Josie Durand, a senior who lived a couple of miles up the road past Miranda's turnoff, gave her a ride home.

Miranda let her parents know she was home and then went to the barn. She greeted each horse by stroking its face and neck She talked to them as she offered a carrot to each one. All but Shooting Star accepted. Miranda got one of the special horse treats that Dr. Talbot had ordered; she refused that, too. She turned her back and stood, head down, in the corner. "I wish I knew what's wrong with you, baby. If I could make you feel better, you know I would."

She felt a hand on her shoulder and spun around, with fists guarding her face.

"Whoa. Don't hit me." Chris said, stepping back. "I just wanted to welcome you home."

"Oh. I'm so sorry. I guess I'm just awfully jumpy—what with two madmen after me."

"Two?"

"Hicks, of course. But I think Dennis is worse. I just wish he'd leave me alone." Miranda led Chris back to the bed in the alleyway where he'd been sleeping, so they could both sit down. She told him everything that had happened on tour.

Chris jumped up red-faced and fists clinched. "Wait until I get my hands on the..."

"He swears he'll get even," Miranda interrupted. "He's probably just bluffing. I think he's a coward at heart; but, still, I don't trust him. I'm seriously thinking of quitting choir."

"If you like choir—and you are the best singer I've ever heard—I don't think you should let him win."

"Win?"

"Yeah. If you give up what you love because you're scared of him, he's won."

"I'm not scared of him. Well, maybe a little. I just don't like him. But you're right. I'll stay in choir—and the Harmonics."

"If he touches you again, I'll kill him, Miranda. I'm serious. I'll be watching him." Chris was pacing.

"I don't want you in trouble over him. He's not worth it. Maybe I should tell the principal."

"You probably should." Chris plunked down on her bed and then stood up again. "I guess I'd better get home so you can have your bed," Chris said, standing.

"No. You go ahead and sleep here. I'll go in the house to sleep. Be sure to lock the door after me."

When Miranda crept into the bedroom she shared with Margot, a light turned on. Margot sat up in bed, squinting.

"Sorry. I didn't mean to wake you," Miranda said.

"I wanted to give you this," Margot said, holding out a large, bright-red envelope. "I think it's a Christmas card, but I want to know who's sending you personal cards. It's from a boy.

Miranda took the card and looked at the return address. "Teddy H.H., Crow Agency, MT."

Miranda grinned and ripped it open. "Yeah it's from my new boyfriend. My hero, actually," she teased.

Dear Miranda. Mom says we can come see you after Christmas, if it's okay with you. Please let us come, okay? Teddy.

There was a note folded inside from his grandmother.

We don't want to be an imposition, but Teddy has been bugging me ruthlessly. His latest is to say that Rising Sun is in big trouble and he needs to get there soon. I asked how he knew this and he just thumped his chest and said, "My heart tells me the truth."

If it is all right, we'll come up the day after Christmas and stay two or three days. That means we'll need lodging. Will you recommend a hotel nearby?

Lucille.

P.S. Teddy insists that he will fast and pray until he sees Rising Sun. I can't get him to eat, so please let us come.

"You're in luck, Margot. You'll get to meet him. He and his grandmother want to come visit after Christmas."

"What's he like, Miranda?"

"You'll see. Now go to sleep."

"I can't. Now that you have my curiosity up I'll never go to sleep."

So Miranda described Teddy and told Margot details about the cave in the mountains and all that Teddy did to save her.

"Is he in love with you?"

"Don't be silly. He's ten years old. He's in love with my horse, Shooting Star. He calls her Rising Sun and she's the one he's coming to see, not me."

Miranda lay awake for some time, wondering what he meant about Star being in trouble. How could he possibly know that she was sick, losing weight, and unresponsive to everything they did for her? Is that what he meant? Or did he know something she didn't. He seemed to have a sixth sense about things.

Miranda lay awake until almost time to get up, and then she slept so soundly that she overslept. She woke up when Margot came in and shook her by the shoulder. "Chris is in the kitchen. He's ready to leave, but if he waits for you, he'll be late for school."

"What time is it?" Miranda asked in alarm. "Why didn't you wake me earlier?"

"I tried. Three times."

"Okay. Tell Chris to wait. I'll be right there," Miranda said as she stripped off her pajamas and grabbed her jeans from the floor."

"Too late. Dad just sent him on to school. He said he'd drive you," Margot said after running to the kitchen and back. "He said there is no sense in both of you being late. Chris said he already put the horses out and started cleaning stalls. He'll help with the rest after school."

"Shouldn't you be on the bus?"

"I missed it. Dad's going to drop me off, too."

The bell was ringing when Dad's truck stopped in front of the school. Margot jumped out and ran to the elementary side of the building. Miranda gathered her books, thanked her father for the ride, and hurried to the main door to the high school.

"Shut your dirty mouth, Dennis," she heard Chris yell from around the corner.

"Ha, ha. You are so jealous that you never got to experience the kind of passion she showed me. Wow, that girl's good in a hay loft!"

She rounded the corner in time to see Chris's fist connect with Dennis's jaw. Dennis fell, and Chris jumped on top of him, continuing to pound Dennis's face.

"Stop it, Christopher Bergman. Get off that boy right now!" shouted the vice-principal, Mr. Gammick, who came running from behind Miranda. Chris didn't stop until Mr. Gammick grabbed him. Mr. Mooney, the boys' coach and gym teacher, joined him and together they pulled Chris to his feet.

"Take him to the office," Gammick told the coach. "I'll get Dennis to the infirmary and call his parents. I think he'll need to see a doctor."

Dennis's face was bleeding, and he was crying. Miranda stared until Mr. Gammick saw her and shouted, "Why aren't you in class, Miss Stevens. I'll talk with you later."

Chris looked at her with an embarrassed grin and shrugged his shoulders as Gammick led him away.

She wanted to talk to him and trotted along beside him for a moment, but the coach roared. "If you aren't in class in one minute, you may be facing suspension, too."

Miranda turned toward the music room.

Chapter Twenty-six

As Miranda mucked out stalls, she listened for Chris's truck to pull into the yard. It never came. Leaving Queen until last, she brought in all the horses and made sure they each had hay. She gave each one a carrot. Shooting Star, took hers with seeming reluctance like a petulant child saying, "Fine, if it makes you happy, but I'm really not interested." She moved away from Miranda's hand to stand, head down, in her corner.

Miranda sighed and went back for Queen. "Hey, beautiful girl, where is your boy? I hope they didn't send him to jail. He doesn't deserve it. I can only guess what Dennis is telling them."

Queen's head went up and down vigorously, as if she were seconding Miranda's words. "Yeah, you agree? What you're really saying is 'hurry up and get me my dinner,' huh?" Miranda laughed, patted Queen's neck, and led her inside. She gave Queen two carrots, as if that would make up for whatever Chris was going through.

As Miranda walked back to the house, she thought about the fight. Dennis looked pretty bad, but she felt no sympathy. "I hate you, Dennis, and I'll hate you even more if Chris gets in trouble for this," she muttered.

Neither Chris nor Dennis were at school the next day. Rumors flew everywhere about the "terrible fight."

Miranda was in a stall in the girls' bathroom when some of her classmates came in. "Chris has a vicious temper. I hope I never do some little thing to tick him off," she heard Stephanie say.

"I wonder if Dennis will be okay. Someone said Chris broke his nose." Miranda recognized Lisa's voice.

"That's a shame. Dennis has a beautiful nose," Tammy said. "He's the handsomest guy in the school. I will hate Chris if he spoiled that."

"You're so in love with Dennis, Tam," another voice piped in. One of the sophomore girls had come in to join the conversation.

Miranda kept listening, silently seething.

"What was the fight about?" the sophomore asked.

"Who knows? Chris has plenty of reasons to be jealous of Dennis. Looks, money, his car, and his way with girls. Maybe they were fighting over Miranda."

Miranda couldn't handle hearing any more gossip. She flushed the toilet and walked out, slamming the stall door. "Excuse me. May I get to the sink, please?"

"Oh, Miranda. I didn't know you were in here," Tammy said.

"Obviously!" Miranda said.

"Well, what we said was all true, wasn't it?" Lisa challenged.

"No. It's not. Because you don't know anything about it. But you decide who's guilty and who's not. Whatever made Chris mad enough to hit someone had to be pretty bad, so why don't you get your facts before you start making judgments?"

"Way to go, Miranda. Stick up for your loser boyfriend," Stephanie said.

Kimberly said, "Careful, Steph. Don't forget Miranda has a worse temper than Chris. If you're not careful, you'll be next."

Miranda shook her head and started to leave. She recognized that she had a temper, and it was a constant fight to contain it. Still, she couldn't resist. She turned and lunged at the girls who were still staring at her. With hands like claws and teeth bared, she let out a lion-like roar. They all jumped back, screaming.

Stephanie shrieked. "Oh, my gosh. What a freak! She could've killed us."

Miranda turned and walked down the hall, smiling and shaking her head.

Laurie found her and asked, "Ready for lunch?"

"No, you go ahead. I'm going to skip it today. I need to find out what's happening with Chris."

"Want me to go with you?"

"No. You eat. I'll meet you at choir practice."

Mrs. Bergman sat behind the checkout counter reading a magazine when Miranda walked into the general store. She looked up with an artificial smile on her bright red lips. The smile disappeared instantly when she saw Miranda. Her eyes narrowed and her lower jaw protruded in a pout.

"You are not welcome here, young lady. Get out!"

Miranda stopped, stunned for a moment, until anger took the place of her shock. "Oh, sorry. I thought this establishment was open to the public. I didn't see any signs."

Mrs. Bergman rose to her feet. "Don't get smart with me, young lady. I own this store, and I'll say who can come in and who can't."

"Where's Chris?" Miranda asked.

"It's none of your business where he is. He won't be seeing you again." Mrs. Bergman leaned over the counter and glared at Miranda. "You, young lady, are nothing but trouble."

Okay, Miranda thought. *I think we've established that I'm a young lady. Of course, it could be a lot worse.*

"For how long?" she asked.

"Forever, that's how long! We've had enough of your bad influence on my son. All the trouble he's ever gotten into has been your fault."

Miranda doubted that, but said nothing.

"Fighting over a wild, spoiled, indecent girl! I never thought I'd see the day!" Mrs. Bergman shook her head and rapidly blinked her eyes.

Okay, I liked "young lady" better, Miranda thought. Still she didn't say anything, hoping Mrs. Bergman would go on. She did. "Can you imagine what everyone in the community will think of us when they hear that our son is suspended from school for a week? His name is blackened and ours along with it." Mrs. Bergman looked close to tears. "Well, you can bet he's going to work his tail off and not set a foot on your place. As for you, young lady,"—*Oh good! We're back to "young lady.*—"he won't be going to your house to do chores and whatever else you two do over there. We're looking for another place to board his horse."

"What about Star?"

"Who?"

"Shooting Star. She's half his, you know. And she needs lots of special attention. She's sick," Miranda said. "Shall we divide custody? Have her stay with Queen half the time and Starlight the other half?"

Miranda enjoyed seeing the consternation on Mrs. Bergman's face—until it changed to rage.

"Get out! Now, before I call the cops," she yelled and picked up the phone.

Miranda wasn't sure if she could be arrested for anything, but she had all the information she'd come for. She smiled, said, "Have a nice day," and backed out the door. As she walked away, she heard a tapping sound. She turned and saw Chris in an upstairs window. He kissed his fingers and waved to her. He gave her his brightest smile and a big thumbs up.

Laurie started coming regularly, riding the bus home with Miranda to help with the chores. She'd always helped take care of her horses, but sometimes let a day or two go by when Miranda and Chris would do them all, saying she'd make it up to them later, by doing some of theirs. "I'll come stay with you over Christmas vacation, if that's okay with your parents," Laurie said.

"You don't have to go to Cincinnati?"

"No, they kind of want me to, but I convinced them that I needed to be here to help, and I would really be bored in Ohio. There are no kids in the family my age, and Grandma doesn't even recognize anyone anymore."

"I'm so glad you get to stay. We'll have a great time. You can meet Teddy and his Grandmother."

Mr. Flanders entered the choir room with a frown on his face Wednesday morning. He looked at Miranda when he said, "Just before the Christmas program, we lose our tenor soloist. Now, what do we do?"

Miranda was quiet, but when Mr. Flanders kept staring at her, she asked, "Are you asking me?"

"I'm asking all of you. You realize, of course, that due to a schoolyard brawl, Dennis has become incapacitated and will not be able to perform with us."

"Do you think that's my fault?"

"I didn't say that, but if the shoe fits..."

"I didn't start any fight. And I don't know what you expect me to do."

Miranda's whole body tingled with embarrassment and the surprise of such a personal attack. How dare he embarrass her in front of the whole choir.

"How bad is Dennis hurt?" one of the girls asked. "I saw him in the hall this morning.

"He's back in school, but he simply can't sing with a split lip and a broken nose. So, I had to excuse him from choir."

Miranda's humiliation smoldered into anger. She thought of getting up, leaving, and telling the stupid teacher that she quit. That would serve him right.

Laurie put a hand on Miranda's arm and leaned in close to whisper, "Don't let Flanders get to you. He's acting surprisingly like a jerk. Don't take it personally."

Miranda didn't say anything, but she took a deep breath and thought about it. This was a side of Flanders she'd never seen before. She didn't know what his problem was, but she wouldn't punish herself for his meanness. She loved singing and really looked forward to performing for her family and friends tonight.

"Who among you thinks he can take over Dennis's aria?" Flanders asked.

No one spoke or raised a hand. Miranda nudged Laurie. "You could," she whispered. "Who says it has to be a boy?"

"You think so?" Laurie looked pleased.

"Do you girls have something to say to the whole group? If not..." Flanders began.

"Yes," Laurie said, standing. "I want to volunteer to take Dennis's place. I know the aria well, and I've sung it at home."

Mr. Flanders visibly jerked back in surprise. He looked around the room as if to find a better alternative. Slowly shaking his head, he finally said. "Okay. Let's hear it. We'll start with the movement just before it, and we'll see how you do. Do you need a copy of the words?"

"No, I'm sure I can remember." Laurie smiled and squeezed Miranda's hand. "Wish me luck."

"Those of you who are not in the chamber choir just sit and listen." Mr. Flanders nodded to the pianist and then raised his baton.

When they came to Dennis's part, Laurie didn't hesitate, but sang strongly and naturally. It was prettier than any time Dennis had sung it.

"Well done," Mr. Flanders said. "I should have given it to you all along."

Miranda managed to get through all of her classes without losing her temper and saying anything unkind to the girls all around her who went on and on about "poor Dennis." She found it easier than she'd anticipated to avoid him. He was always surrounded by girls offering him sympathy, touching his bruised lip, and asking if his swollen black eye hurt very much. "He's still handsome. He looks mysterious with that black eye," Kimberly said.

Miranda's whole family, including her grandparents, seemed more excited than Miranda as they drove to the school for the Christmas program. Their small-town school housed students from kindergarten through twelfth grade. The Christmas program was always long because the junior high and high school music students performed after the elementary kids. Of course, Margot and Elliot had parts in the Christmas play, which came first in the program. The Harmonics would be last after the high school band. Some of the older people from the community as well as parents with young children, left before the band and choir performances.

Elliot was the star of the play, and he did a beautiful job of it, bringing tears of joy and pride to Miranda's eyes as she watched. Margot did just as well.

When it was finally her turn to go up to the stage, Grandpa, who was sitting next to her, gave her a one-armed hug and kissed the top of her head. "Just enjoy yourself, Mandy. You'll make us proud."

There was a standing ovation after the performance and Flanders led them in "Silver Bells" which they'd practiced with the whole choir. After it was over, Miranda shared the limelight with Laurie, who was getting as many compliments as she was. It made Miranda happy, especially when some stranger suggested that they should team up and sing a duet for the talent show. When Miranda saw Dennis coming toward her, she backed up and escaped into the crowd. She wasn't going to let him spoil an otherwise fantastic day.

She looked for Chris in the crowd, but evidently his parents didn't let him come. They weren't there, either.

On Friday, the last day of school before vacation, Laurie met Miranda as she got off the bus. "I have good news and bad news," she said. "Which do you want first?"

"Well, let's get the bad news out of the way first. Then the good news can cheer me up."

Laurie took a deep breath and said, "I can't stay with you after all. My mom changed her mind."

"Oh, no. Why?"

"Big change of plans. My aunt says not to come to Ohio because Grandma doesn't want any company, and they are going to Chicago for Christmas. Then my Uncle Manuel called from California and asked us to come to his place. Rose Marie will be there, so I have to go. It will be nice to see her, but I'd rather stay with you. I don't think it's fair to leave you with all the chores to do."

"Oooh," Miranda whined. "I was really looking forward to spending all of Christmas vacation with you. But don't worry about the chores. Margot and Elliot will help." Miranda tried to sound cheerful. "Tell Rose Marie 'hi' for me. I hope she's doing okay. I should get her a present for you to take."

Laurie's cousin, Rose Marie, was older than Laurie and Miranda by about four years. She'd lived with Laurie's family during her senior year of high school. There'd been a time when Miranda considered her an enemy, but they'd finally become friends before Rose Marie moved back to California to go to college.

"Okay, I'm ready for the good news," Miranda said.

Laurie handed a small box, wrapped in silver paper with a bright blue bow on top.

"Hey, I thought we'd agreed we weren't going to buy each other presents this year."

"Not from me," Laurie said with a grin.

"Then who's it from?"

"It's from Chris. I went to the store the day his mother has bridge club, and Chris was there. He asked me to give it to you. Are you going to open it?"

Miranda opened the note that was taped to the box. "Don't open until Christmas. And only when you are alone with the horses!"

"I guess not," Miranda said, smiling.

Chapter Twenty-seven

Miranda didn't get to the barn to go to bed until very late on Christmas Eve. It was always a special family time. They enjoyed games, stories, popcorn and fudge, and ended the evening around the piano as Mom played and everyone sang. Tonight Margot played the piano, too. Miranda knew she took lessons, but was surprised at how well she played. Elliot was learning to play the guitar, so he played along with her. With continuing requests for more songs, no one paid attention to the time until Kort fell off his chair, sound asleep. Then they all hurried to bed.

Miranda visited all of the horses, petting and talking to each one. She lingered a long time with Shooting Star, stroking her, and singing some of the songs she'd just shared with her family. "You must get well, my beautiful horse. You have a very important visitor coming to see you the day after tomorrow. Please be well for him."

Tears came to Miranda's eyes as she said good night and gave Star a hug. The horse responded by leaning against her and heaving a sigh. "I wish I knew what was wrong. You seem very sad. Are you in pain? How I wish you could talk to me. I love you so much."

Miranda looked at the alarm clock beside her bed when she got to the tack room. Midnight. "Hey. It's

Christmas. I can open your gift, Chris. I'm sorry I didn't get you one." She stopped for a minute. "It better not be expensive jewelry like a ring or something, or I'll just have to give it back to you," she said, talking out loud, as if Chris could hear her.

It was a small box and weighed hardly anything, so she was half scared to open it. If it was a ring, she'd kill him. He ought to know... She pulled off the lid and gasped. "Oh, I love it, Chris. You do know me, don't you?" She pulled out the note first.

> *Miranda, I've been studying up on medicine bags and decided to make you one. I even did all the beading myself. I hope you like it. I only put one thing in it. A quartz crystal. It will give you good energy and insight according to what I've read. "It will connect you to your spiritual self." You can decide what else should go in it. It is for you and you only to know what's inside of it.*
>
> *Love, Chris*

Miranda carefully lifted the ornate bag from the box. It was made from very soft leather bound with rawhide. The many-colored bead work on the front formed the shape of a four-pointed star with the lower point elongated, just like the white mark of Shooting Star's forehead. She tried to imagine Chris sitting for a long time with a needle and thread doing the intricate beading. The whole bag was about three inches long and one and a half inches wide with another two inches of fringe made by cutting the same soft leather into tiny strips. It was gathered at the top with a long leather thong so she could wear it around her neck.

Miranda put it on and then lay back on her bed, staring into the darkness, fingering the bag and the crystal inside it. At first her thoughts were on Chris, his kindness, his sense of humor, and how he often surprised her with a thoughtfulness that she supposed was beyond him. Then she thought of Shooting Star, how sad she'd seemed tonight. Miranda had thought of her attitude as sullen. But tonight it just seemed sad. She had tucked her head in against Miranda's back as she leaned into her, as if asking for sympathy and comfort.

She thought of the letter from Lucille. What did Teddy mean about Star being in trouble? How did he know? Evidently his grandmother took it seriously.

Unable to sleep, she walked back to Shooting Star's stall. The filly stood, facing the corner, apparently sleeping. Miranda reached in and plucked a hair from her tail. She slowly wound it around two fingers and then tied the loop with another tail hair. Holding the little bundle to the light, it gleamed like a new penny with golden highlights. She put it in her medicine bag.

When she awakened the next morning, instead of the usual excitement for Christmas, Miranda felt a strange heaviness in her chest. She couldn't explain it. Worry? Dread? It was much like the feeling of impending doom she'd had before the Crow Fair last summer. *It's just because I read what Teddy said,* she thought. He was worried, so she was worried, too. And who wouldn't be if they saw Star. That was another thing to worry about. They'd be here tomorrow. She had a lot to do to get ready for them, including sprucing up Shooting Star as much as possible.

Miranda wore her medicine bag as she worked in the barn, leading the horses to their paddocks. Mom called to let her know breakfast was ready as she cleaned the box stall for the little guys. The feeling of impending doom had been growing ever since she woke up.

"I'm going to finish up and put the horses back before I come in, Mom. Go ahead without me," she yelled at the intercom.

She'd just moved on to the next stall when the door opened and Dad walked in.

"Let me give you a hand if you're set on getting this all done before we eat. The kids are waking up and will want to open presents soon. Is that why you are in such a rush to get it all done?"

"I just don't want to leave the horses outside while we eat."

"But we always do that."

"Yes, but we'll be busy inside and won't be able to keep watch. I just have a bad feeling about it."

"Okay. I can't see that anything has changed except that it's Christmas, but I believe that listening to your feelings is a good idea."

With Dad's help, it didn't take long and the horses were soon back in their stalls, munching on hay. Miranda made sure both doors to the stable were locked.

Everyone had eaten, but Mom had saved a plate for

Dad and Miranda. They took them to the living room where they could eat while watching the little guys tackle their gifts. "That's a pretty cool ornament you're wearing, Miranda. Is that what they call a medicine bag?" Dad asked.

"Yep. Chris gave it to me. He made it himself."

"Wow. I had no idea he was such a craftsman."

"Me either," Miranda said, smiling as she fingered the soft leather bag.

After all the gifts were opened and the mess cleaned up, Dad and Miranda went back outside. He hooked the gooseneck horse van to the ranch truck and pulled it to the front door of the barn. Because there was no commercial lodging within sixty miles of their place, they'd offered to let Lucille and Teddy stay in their camper. Once Dad got it situated and leveled, he pulled the pickup away from it and left Miranda to make sure it was clean, the beds made, and extra blankets and towels in place. Dad filled the water tanks, turned on the water heater, and plugged in the two power cords: one for the interior electricity and one for the heat tape around the water pipes.

When Miranda was satisfied that everything was in order for her guests, she went to the barn and put a halter on Shooting Star. She got her to eat some carrots while she gently brushed Star's dark red coat. Once so shiny, it was now rather dull. She kept singing or talking to her, but not all the grooming in the world was going to make her look healthy. She just wasn't. She was downright skinny. Her ribs showed and her backbone was a sharp ridge dividing gaunt flanks, but maybe, with her mane and tail clean, combed and neatly braided, she at least looked as if someone loved her.

Lucille and Teddy arrived at about sundown. Miranda invited them in the house to introduce them to everyone. It was obvious, though, that Teddy only wanted to see Shooting Star. Elliot noticed, too, and offered to take him to the barn. Miranda quietly excused herself to go with them.

"I'd like to see the horses, too," Lucille said, pulling on her coat. No one seemed to want to be left behind and soon the whole family was following. Miranda wished they'd all stay in the house, but she couldn't stop them.

Teddy went straight to Shooting Star, passing by the other horses, and speaking words that she could not understand. Star jerked her head up and faced them. She nickered softly, put her head over the stall door, and lowered her face to Teddy's level as he approached.

He opened the gate and squeezed in past her, hugging her neck. She stepped back and pressed her forehead into his chest while he stroked her face, neck, and ears. He picked up a handful of her nutritional treats from her feeder and fed them to her one by one. She mouthed them from his palm and chewed contentedly. He gave her more and she continued to eat.

Miranda could hardly believe her eyes. Star didn't seem to notice anyone but Teddy. She seemed happy for the first time since the fair. Miranda's first thought was that he had put some kind of spell on her horse. She'd come to think that Teddy actually had magic powers. But then she remembered the time Starlight had been just as sick. They had been separated for the first time since they'd met, and both of them languished. He'd responded in the same way when she came to him, perking up and eating when no one else had been able to get him to. *It's limerence in action,* she told herself, surprised. *I guess horses can feel it, too.*

Lucille watched her grandson with a measure of pride on her face. She turned to Miranda's mom and asked, "Are all of these horses yours?"

"Not mine," Mom said. "Most are Miranda's but not all. Let me introduce them. You've met Shooting Star, who belongs to Miranda and her friend, Christopher, jointly."

"Oh, yes. I remember. You call her Shooting Star. Teddy calls her Rising Sun."

"Both are pretty names," Mom said. "And here we have Queen, Shooting...er, Rising Sun's mother. She belongs to Christopher. The sire is Miranda's Starlight. That's him in this stall."

They wandered on as Mom recited the name and owner of each horse.

"Sunny's mine," Elliot said, joining them and reaching in to pet his mare. The others followed.

Miranda stayed with Teddy, watching. She could almost see the love arcing through the air between them. Finally, Teddy patted Shooting Star and said. I'll be back in a minute." He muttered something in his Crow language and turned to Miranda. "I will look at your horses now." *As if Shooting Star isn't mine?*

"You sleep in the barn?" he asked when they came to the bed at the end of the alley.

"Yes. This is where I sleep every night."

"Hmm," he murmured.

Miranda thought she heard envy in his voice. *He probably wants my bed as well as my horse. Well, too bad. I'm not giving up either one.*

When he'd seen all the horses he went back to Star.

"Teddy, Mrs. Stevens has invited us to eat with them," Lucille said. "Come. You must be hungry. It's time to end your fast."

Teddy sighed, patted Star on the muzzle, and spoke to her again in Crow.

Mom had been keeping dinner warm since before Lucille and Teddy arrived. They all gathered around the table and enjoyed the roast beef, mashed potatoes, carrots, green beans, and salad. Everyone was quite hungry by then, so there wasn't much talk as the food disappeared. Miranda and Margot cleared the dirty dishes, and Margo brought out a big chocolate cake she'd baked and frosted that afternoon.

After dessert, Lucille insisted on helping with the dishes and cleaning up the kitchen. While Miranda helped, Elliot and Teddy went back to the barn. It made her nervous to have the boys out there without the door locked. What if Hicks chose this time to come? Mom seemed to understand her distress and told her to go on out to the barn with the boys.

She wondered why she was suddenly so worried

about Hicks. If he hadn't shown up after all these months, he probably wasn't going to. Yet that feeling she'd had all day was not gone.

"Teddy, come to the camper with me," Lucille called a few minutes later. "It's time for us to let these good people go to bed—and get some sleep ourselves so you can spend a full day tomorrow with your horse." She looked at Miranda quickly and said, "Your favorite horse, I mean. Not that she's yours."

"May I sleep in the barn with her? I could put a sleeping bag on the floor in her stall."

"No. You may not. Tell Rising Sun goodnight."

Teddy shot a furtive glance at Miranda, as if she could help him get what he wanted. She ignored it.

"Elliot," she said, "you better go back to the house."

Little Brother, who usually slept beside Miranda's bed, wagged his tail and trotted after Teddy when he went out. "You, too?" Miranda muttered. "Traitor."

She double-locked the door behind them and prepared for bed. She needed to go in and brush her teeth and wash her face, but she didn't want to leave the barn. It seemed like a safe haven that she especially needed tonight. So she put on her pajamas and crawled under the covers. She lay awake for a long time before finally drifting into a fitful sleep.

Chapter Twenty-eight

The soft, low-pitched woof that Miranda knew as Little Brother's let's-go-play bark sounded just outside the tack room window. She swung her legs out of bed, stepped into her snow boots, and went to open the door. *Teddy must have left him outside and now he wants in,* Miranda thought. But when she opened the door he was nowhere in sight. She peeked around the corner just in time to see a figure disappear around the corner of the barn.

She jumped back and closed the door, leaning against the wall as she let her heart slow down. A dark figure moving across the white snow, dimly lit by moonlight had given her a start. *It's just Teddy.* She realized. *What the heck could he be up to in the middle of the night?*

She grabbed her parka, slipping it over her flannel pajamas as she went out the door. She hurried around the corner of the barn where she'd seen him disappear, thankful for the soft snow that muted the sound of her footsteps. Looking across the big corral, she saw Little Brother bounding through the deep snow in the moonlight. Teddy straggled behind. Miranda followed the tracks, catching up with him as he reached the loafing shed where snow sliding from the roof had piled up to the eaves. Teddy climb it and she followed. When he turned to call Little Brother to come up, he saw her.

"Why did you follow me?" he asked, not sounding the least bit happy to see her.

"To find out what you are doing out here in the middle of the night. Why aren't you sleeping?"

"I came here to be alone to pray," Teddy said accusingly.

"You can pray. I won't bother you. I'll sit at the other end of the roof if it makes you feel better."

Teddy seemed to think about this for a few moments. "It's okay. You can stay."

"Why are you wearing warpaint? You look like you're ready for the fair."

"I couldn't sleep," Teddy said, quietly. "The bed over the table in the camper is not very comfortable."

"I would think it's a little more comfortable than the stone floor of a cave."

Teddy grinned at this. "It's soft enough. It's just that it's inside with no fresh air. Besides that, I felt kind of sick. I think I ate too much."

"So?"

"I kept thinking about your big, black dog."

"Little Brother."

"Yes. He tried to follow me inside, but Grandmother said, 'No..' I felt like I had betrayed his trust. I didn't want to leave him lying in the cold all by himself."

"So you got up to see about him, but that doesn't explain the lines on your face." Miranda said.

Teddy shook his head at Miranda's questions, but went on. "I told you in the cave, I want to be like the last great warrior and chief of the Crows. He is my great-great grandfather, and I believe I am supposed to be like him. He was wise because the spirits talked to him and gave him messages for his people. I went to the mountains and the spirits talked to me, too. Tonight, I prayed some more—about my sadness for the horse and the dog who wanted to be with me." Teddy paused so long Miranda thought he was finished, but he hadn't answered her question. Finally, he went on. "Before I left home, I had a dream—a vision. I was in warpaint, and I was counting coups on an enemy. It was a man I don't know, but he had to be stopped. My dream showed me that I am the one who must stop him."

Miranda raised her eyebrows, thinking that was kind of egotistical. She said, "But it was just a dream. Right?"

"I think it means something."

As Miranda stared at his earnest face. "To put on war paint?" she asked.

Teddy grinned, looking slightly embarrassed. "Yes. According to my dream. But I didn't have warpaint, and that worried me, but again Akbaatatdia gave me an answer. My grandmother left her makeup on the edge of the sink. I used her lipstick to make lines down my face. Red is a good color for war paint. I used her mascara to go between the red lines. Black is for victory."

"Well, it's pretty impressive. If you met someone in the dark, they'd probably scream and run."

From their rooftop perch, they looked out at the silhouette of the mountains, the glint of the moon on the river, and occasional car lights on the highway. Miranda followed Teddy's gaze and looked up at the sky. Her knees ached from squatting, so she sat and stretched out her legs. When the cold penetrated her pajamas, she stood and looked out across the barnyard. A light twinkled in the distance along the road from town. She watched it flicker as it passed behind some trees. It disappeared for a while and then appeared again, closer.

"That car turned onto the road that goes by our house. Kind of strange for this time of night."

Teddy stood and looked where she pointed. "Why is that strange?"

"Our neighbors down the road are old. They don't go out at night unless something is wrong."

"Listen. I can hear it," Teddy said. Miranda heard the motor as the lights moved slowly up the hill, stopped, and went out. The motor went silent and a car door slammed.

"A funny place to park a car," Miranda whispered. They kept watching, but it was too dark to see the vehicle or anyone who might have gotten out of it.

In a few minutes, Little Brother raised his head and his ears pricked forward. He rumbled a low growl.

"We'd better go see," Teddy said quietly. He lowered climbed down and strode toward the barn and the camper/trailer, making no sound. He put his hand on Little Brother's collar to quiet him and keep him from running ahead. Miranda followed just as quietly.

They were in the deep shadow of the trailer when a dark form loomed between them and the barn door. Teddy stiffened, and Miranda's heart leapt into her throat. A gun aimed at the barn glinted in the moonlight. Hicks! She couldn't see his face, but she'd never forget his dark figure. Her horses! She'd forgotten to lock the door.

Before she could decide what to do, Teddy spoke in a deep, confident voice "Who are you?"

The man jumped back and let out a guttural yelp. He looked around, swinging his gun in front of him.

"Stop!" Teddy said, Making his deep voice, deeper, louder. He stayed in the shadow of the camper and Miranda didn't think Hicks could see either of them.

"Please put your gun on the ground," Teddy said.

"No way! Show yourself first," Hicks squeaked. "I mean it. Step out and show yourself. I won't shoot." He pulled the ski mask off his face and stared wildly in Teddy's direction, apparently unable to see him. "Who are you?" he asked, his voice tinged with panic.

"I am Theodore Hungry Horse," Teddy intoned, "Chief of the Apsáalooke. I come in the company of Awakkulé and Akbaatatdia. Put down your gun."

"Who? Chief of what?" the man asked, confusion showing on his bristled face. "With who?"

"Akbaatatdia, the One who has made everything. And Awakkulé, the Little People of the Pryor Mountains. They will not be happy if you do not put down your gun."

"Let me see you, all of you, or I'll shoot."

Miranda reached for Teddy to hold him back, but

his nylon jacket slipped from her hands as he stepped from the shadow of the trailer into the moonlight. Hicks shrieked and stepped backward, tripping over the foot scraper and landing flat on his back next to the barn door. He dropped the gun when he fell.

Teddy stepped forward.

The man's eyes widened, and he scooted backward on his elbows. "Please don't hurt me. I know who you are. I read stories about Little People and their powers."

"Who are you?" Teddy asked. "And why do you have a gun?"

"I'm, uh, my name is..."

"Tell the truth."

"Martin. Martin Hicks. I am here to see a girl, a girl and her devil horse."

"Why did you bring a gun?"

Hicks felt around with his right hand. Not finding the gun, he sat up and saw Teddy standing on it. Hicks leaned forward, reaching for Teddy's leg. A snarl escaped his lips as his face contorted into an evil grin. Miranda leapt forward, but not before Little Brother growled and lunged, teeth bared. He landed on Hicks's chest.

"Bear!" Hicks screeched and scooted backward, crablike. "Somebody stop the bear. Get it off me!"

Miranda was stunned by the man's shrill shrieks, especially when he began sobbing hysterically.

Teddy stepped back and picked up the gun as Little Brother continued a low rumbling growl at Hicks.

"You meant to kill the horse and the girl?" Teddy asked.

"They hurt me. That black devil tried to kill me! I have to get him." Hicks whined.

"Akbaatatdia says revenge is wrong," Teddy said. "Would you want to feel God's vengeance?"

"No. Don't hurt me. Call off the bear! Don't let him kill me." Hicks's eyes never left Little Brother, and he didn't even try to move, as if every muscle was frozen. "Please. You can control the bear. I know you have magic powers. Please help me," Hicks burbled on, "You could help me. I heard that, too. I heard you sometimes have mercy. Please!"

"I have no magic. I don't believe in magic. I have helpers. And they have greater power than you or your gun. I'll call off the bear if you will get on your knees and close your eyes," Teddy said.

Hicks flipped onto his knees, scrambled to his feet, turned to run. Little Brother growled and grabbed his pants' leg. Hicks stopped.

"Get the bear off me," he screamed. "I'll do what you say." Hicks turned, dropped to his knees in front of Teddy, and covered his face with both arms.

Teddy handed the gun to Miranda.

Holding it gingerly by the pearl handle, she thought it looked like a toy replica of the six-shooters she'd seen in old western movies. But this gun was heavy and deadly. She carefully laid it beneath the trailer.

Teddy stood over Hicks and began singing an eerie chant in his native tongue. He sang for a long time. Little Brother pressed against him, joining in with a mournful howl. Miranda watched in amazement, as Hicks leaned lower and lower until his forehead touched the ground. He wailed along with Teddy's song and Little Brother's baying. It was enough to wake the dead.

Someone touched her arm and Miranda looked around to see Teddy's grandmother beside her. When she looked back, she saw her parents, Margot, Elliot, and her grandparents standing across from her in a semicircle, eyes wide open, not moving, as if they were all holding their breath. She realized she was. Dad had his hunting rifle in his hands. It was aimed at the ground, but she could see he was ready to use it in an instant, if necessary. Mom kept looking from Teddy and Hicks to the road, as if expecting someone.

Teddy stopped singing, but Hicks continued to cry for another minute or two and then slowly sat up. Teddy looked down at him and said. "You came with hate in your heart. Hate will eat you from the inside out. You must let that go."

"I will. I do," Hick said. "I won't hurt the girl. I won't hate her or her devil horse if you won't hurt me."

"I prayed for hatred to be washed from your heart. Is it gone?" Teddy stood over the man, asking the questions with authority.

"Yes," Hicks said. "I don't hate the girl anymore."

Hicks stared at Teddy for a moment. When he saw Teddy looking beyond him, he turned around. Seeing the people behind him, he scooted back toward Teddy. He looked wildly around him, as he slowly got to his knees and then to his feet. When he saw Miranda, he began to cry. "Please forgive me, girl. I was going to shoot you. I got a gun and came here to shoot you and that devil horse dead. I'm sorry. Please forgive me."

Miranda just stood there staring at him. This man was truly crazy. It was a wonder Teddy wasn't dead. She looked at the boy and slowly smiled. "You *are* the chief. This is a miracle if I ever saw one. And being around you, I think I've seen several."

"Better forgive him," Teddy said.

Miranda turned to Hicks who was edging toward her and said something she'd never imagined saying. "I forgive you."

Hicks reached for her hand with both of his, ready, it appeared, to kiss it—maybe even to hug her. She jerked her hand away and stepped backward. Before Hicks could pursue her, headlights illuminated the scene, giving Miranda a good look at Hicks for the first time. He had a short, scraggly beard, small eyes, and wore dirty, ragged clothes. His coat was very thin and his pants had holes in them.

"Aren't you cold?" she asked.

"Freezing," Hicks said.

A car door slammed, and a man in a sheriff's uniform walked into the light from his car headlights.

"Are you Martin Hicks?" he asked the trembling man.

"Yes." Hicks's voice shook.

"You are under arrest. Put your hands behind your back and turn around."

Hicks did as he was told, and the sheriff clamped handcuffs around his wrists and led him to the car.

"There's a gun around here somewhere," Hicks said. "A really cool six-shooter. Ya better find it. I stole it. They might want it back."

"I heard about a stolen gun," the sheriff said. He installed Hicks in the back seat and closed the door. "Anyone know where the gun is?"

"Over here under the trailer," Miranda said.

"I'll get it for you," Teddy said, running to her side.

"No, I'll get it," the sheriff said, walking over with his flashlight. He found the gun on the packed snow, picked it up, opened the revolving cylinder, and emptied it of the two bullets it contained.

The sheriff put his hand on Teddy's shoulder as they walked over to Miranda's family. Shaking his head, he said, "I'm going to have to hear the whole story one of these days. I want to know how a kid captured this dangerous criminal."

Teddy grinned up at him, looking embarrassed and proud at the same time.

Chapter Twenty-nine

Miranda leaned against Star's chest, her arms wrapped around her neck. All the excitement had died down, and Hicks was safely in the arms of the law. Everyone had gone back to bed, but Miranda couldn't begin to go back to sleep.

"Star, baby, why can't you love me like you love Teddy? I have loved you and taken care of you since you were a premature baby. We've had some very good times together, don't you think?" A sob caught in Miranda's throat. She let out a ragged sigh as she reached up and patted the tall filly's neck.

What a night it had been. The emotions that raged inside her ran from relief, awe, sadness, disbelief, and jealousy. Yes, she had to admit it. As much as she admired Teddy, she was jealous that her horse loved him so much that she would pine away for him to the point of starvation—and then brighten up and start eating the minute she saw him. What was it with that kid? Did he actually possess some kind of magic?

She thought of how different things could have turned out if Teddy hadn't been there—if no one had stopped Hicks from shooting through the stable door. As she remembered how Hicks's wailing and Little Brother's howling had melded with Teddy's plaintive song, she wondered if he had known he could bring the big man to his knees? Wasn't he taking a big chance? He could have been shot, yet he seemed confident that the crazy man would fear him. Miranda would ask Lucille about it later.

As she stroked Shooting Star, her tears fell freely. "It seems to me that you have chosen your master, or should I say friend and soul mate? I guess it doesn't matter whose name is on the papers that grant ownership. You're telling me you can't be owned. Just loved." Miranda cried quietly for a few more minutes until she remembered the words that renowned horse trainer, Buck Brannaman, had said to her about Starlight.

"There's more than one way to own a horse," He'd said. "People who think of a horse as a piece of property are content to own the title to him. But people who see a horse as a free spirit know that a horse really belongs to no one except to the one he gives his heart." It had made her very happy to hear that in one way Starlight was already hers because he'd given her his heart. It wasn't so nice to think that a horse she supposedly owned gave her heart to someone else.

"I guess you've made your choice clear, Star. But I really would like another chance. Try to love me, too, can't you?"

Star didn't move other than to let her head sink a little heavier on Miranda's shoulder. Miranda felt a little hopeful until she realized that the filly had fallen asleep.

"Oh, well, I guess I should try to get some sleep, too. Teddy will be here for a couple more days, so we can see if he's the one you really choose to be with. I love you, Star."

After a late breakfast the next morning, Miranda followed Lucille to the camper as Teddy, Elliot, and Margot skipped happily into the barn to begin chores.

"Lucille, may I ask you a serious question?"

"Of course, dear. I'll answer if I can."

"Does Teddy have magic powers?"

"No, of course not. The only powers that he has are ones that are possible for all of us." Lucille answered. "Spiritual powers, is what I call them."

"But I can't do what he does. How did he lift me and get me to the cave when I was unconscious in the mountains? How did he get Hicks to drop his gun and listen to him? How did he make my horse love him so much?"

"I'm not sure how he managed to get you to the cave, but he is strong for a ten-year-old boy. He claims that the Little People gave him the strength. Helped him. Maybe they did. Maybe they lifted you onto the horse. I wasn't there, so I can't say. Maybe the strength was in Teddy, and believing they were there helped him find it." Lucille paused as if deciding how much she should say to a girl who knew so little of her peoples' tradition and history. Finally she added. "I believe what our chief, Plenty Coups, has told us. If they helped him, why not Teddy? No one I know has a truer heart than my grandson."

"So the Little People are real?"

Lucille smiled and rested her hand on Miranda's shoulder. "What do you think, Miranda? I can't say that I've ever seen one or had communication with any. But I don't think that means they do not exist. What a limited life we would have if we only believed in the things we can see and touch."

Miranda nodded, thinking of all the things she believed in that could not be seen. "What about Hicks?" she asked. "I mean what kept him from killing Teddy? I was so afraid he would."

"As you told me last night, Mr. Hicks is mentally ill. When he saw Teddy wearing what the man must have thought was war paint, it terrified him. He must have thought he was seeing spirits. And he's obviously terrified of bears and thought he'd met one face to face. Little Brother was a big help in subduing the man."

"My horse?"

"I don't know. Animals have souls, too, as you know. I've seen horses bond with special people, and I'm sure that you have, too. Your horse and Teddy just seem to be, as we say, kindred spirits."

Later that day, they all went for a ride, Miranda on Starlight; Lucille on Ebony; Mom on Lady with Laurie's permission via a phone call; Dad on Queen with the assumption that Chris wouldn't mind, Elliot on his horse, Sunny; Margot on Sea Foam; and Teddy on Shooting Star or, as he insisted on calling her, Rising Sun. She was still horribly skinny, but she seemed in good spirits, ready to go. Kort rode in front of Dad and Kaden with Mom.

Teddy rode without a saddle. "I don't weigh much, so I don't think she'll get too tired carrying me; if she does, I'll walk."

Miranda kept an eye on them as they rode. Star didn't seem to tire at all. She didn't look one bit fatter than she had when they brought her home from the wolf encounter when she seemed so weak that Miranda had wondered if she'd even make it home. Now, she seemed to have boundless energy, eagerly following the other horses up the trail, passing and leading sometimes.

Again Miranda shook her head and wondered, *How does he do it?*

When they returned from the trail ride up Silver Butte, Lucille thanked them over and over for the ride. "It was beautiful, relaxing, and fun," she said. "And what a horse Ebony is!"

"Yes," Miranda agreed. "More than most people can handle, but you had no trouble with her at all. Both you and Teddy are expert horsemen...er, horse-people."

Lucille smiled, "Perhaps we can come back and visit again. Maybe during spring break.

"Of course. Anytime," Miranda said, and her parents seconded it.

Mom insisted again that Teddy and Lucille join them for supper. Lucille agreed and made them all fry bread, while Mom stirred a pot of chili and Miranda put together a salad. Margot made a pie for dessert.

"I should tell you," Lucille said, as if she just remembered, "the tribal police may have found the men who shot Miranda."

"Really? Who?"

"They just arrested a couple of men for poaching deer on Crow land. The men said they didn't realize they were on the reservation. They were reminded that it wasn't hunting season anywhere in the state, so even if they didn't know where they were, which no one believed, they were still breaking the law. When the arresting officer, who is my cousin, asked if they had been here before, one said yes at the same time the other denied it. So they were questioned further. The guy who'd said yes, hurried to say, 'but it was hunting season, and besides we didn't get anything.'

"'Nothing but a horse and rider?' my cousin asked. The men shut up and stared at each other, looking scared. Finally one said he didn't think so. It was snowing and they couldn't see very well, but they shot at an elk. My cousin asked if they were sure it was an elk. One guy said they thought it was, but it looked like it came apart and then disappeared in the trees."

"Why didn't they go look? They could have found Miranda. Maybe got her to the doctor sooner?" Dad said.

"The police asked them that. They said they didn't think about it being a person on a horse, 'besides,' they said, 'there was a blizzard.' They felt lucky to get back to civilization themselves."

"What kind of men would do such a thing. Leave a child to die so they could get back to shelter?" Mom's voice was filled with indignation.

Lucille just shook her head. "Cowards, I guess. Weak men whom I don't want to know. But the tribal police will probably contact you. See if you want to press charges."

"Well, we should," Mom said.

"Wouldn't do any good," Dad said. "I'm sure they'd deny it if we took them to court, and there is no way to prove anything."

The grownups talked some more about it before asking Miranda what she thought.

"I agree with Dad. It's over and done with, and I'm fine now, thanks to Teddy."

They cleared the table and visited some more before Lucille said, "Oh, look at the time. I didn't realize it was so late. We should leave early in the morning, before daylight."

"What? No, Grandmother," Teddy begged. "Please, can't we stay a couple more days? I don't have school until next Tuesday. I thought we could stay all week."

"I didn't tell you we could stay all week. That was your idea. It has been wonderful, and we can come back. Maybe when you have spring break if it's all right with the Stevenses."

The look on Teddy's face was pure sadness, though he didn't argue. "I'm going to tell Rising Sun good night," Teddy said and turned toward the barn.

Miranda followed Lucille out the door. "Lucille, is it possible for you to wait one more day? I don't want to argue with your plans, but I know my whole family would like for you to stay a little longer. You may feel like you are imposing on us, but you're not. It's the opposite. Teddy is helping with the horses, especially Star. He and

Elliot are becoming friends. Mom really likes you, and you've helped her so much." Miranda stopped to take a deep breath and see if she was making any headway. She noticed some hesitation so she forged on.

"I'm just saying you'd be doing us a favor if you could stay a little longer. I hope I'm not being selfish, I mean, if you really need to go..."

"No, Miranda. Since you put it that way, one more day wouldn't make much difference. I don't have to be back any certain time. But I want at least a couple of days to spend with Teddy. Maybe take him to see his father, if he wants to."

"So you'll stay?"

Teddy came from the barn and met them in front of the camper door where they had stopped to talk.

"What?" Hope filled Teddy's big brown eyes.

"One more day," Lucille said.

Chapter Thirty

Chris wasn't running the general store as Miranda had hoped when it opened at nine o'clock the next morning. Instead, his mother sat behind the counter, frowning over a magazine. Mrs. Bergman looked up when the bells attached to the door jingled. The practiced smile she put on for her customers disappeared when she saw Miranda.

"You! I told you not to come here. Now get out!"

"Mrs. Bergman, I need to talk to you," Miranda said.

"Maybe I don't want to talk to you."

"Please," Miranda said, not moving from her spot near the door.

"I'm listening. Make it quick."

"I'm not your enemy. We probably want the very same things and just don't know it. I know you think I'm a bad person, but I don't know why. I don't know what I've done wrong. I think you should tell me so I can either admit it if you're right, or defend myself if you're not. I won't lie, because I don't. I learned my lesson about lying a few years ago when I first met Starlight. I learned that lying doesn't ever pay and that hiding the truth is the same as lying. So please, what have I done in your eyes that makes you hate me so much?"

"Fine! First of all, you made my son is so infatuated with you that he can't think of anything else. I know enough about human nature, especially the nature of adolescent boys, that I know you are doing more than chores and riding horses when he goes to your house."

"You don't trust your son?"

"I don't trust you, Miranda Stevens. I know how boys are. They can't help themselves when a girl offers herself to them."

"I never offered myself to anyone!" Miranda felt her face burn as anger rose in her chest. "And you must not know your son very well, because he's not like that. I know guys who are. Chris isn't one of them."

"Oh, so you admit fooling around with other guys, just not with my son?" The woman sounded offended.

"Mrs. Bergman, I am not like that. I don't 'fool around' with anyone. And neither does Chris."

"Don't try to tell me that Chris isn't infatuated with you. And you know it, but then you go flirting and making out, and who knows what else, with another boy. So my boy loses his temper and knocks the guy down when he brags about it. And Chris is the one who gets suspended from school and gives our family a bad name, not to mention embarrassing himself so that I don't know how he will ever hold his head up in school when they let him back in. You are the one he should have been angry with."

"How can you believe that, Mrs. Bergman? I never did anything with that boy. He made passes at me, and I rejected him. That made him mad, so he lied about it. I hate Dennis, not just for trying to get me alone while we were on tour, but for the kind of person he is. One night, not long ago, he tricked Chris into thinking I asked him to drive me home in his fancy car."

Miranda now stood in front of the checkout counter, looking into Mrs. Bergman's eyes. "Here's what happened that night, just so you know what kind of person your son punched out the other day." A combination of anger and tears made it hard to talk, but she told Mrs. Bergman every detail of that night in Dennis's car, including the lies he'd told Chris to make him leave.

"Does Chris know about this?"

"Yes, I told him later. He was barely speaking to me because he believed Dennis. When I told him what really happened he wanted to beat Dennis up right then. I talked him out of it. Then when I got home from tour, I told Chris what a jerk Dennis was on tour. So when Dennis bragged to him about things that never happened, Chris slugged him. He was defending me."

"So, are you telling me that nothing has ever happened between you and Dennis on tour or any other time? What about Chris? Tell me the truth. Has anything ever happened between you and my son?"

"A lot has happened between Chris and me. But nothing bad."

"No inappropriate necking or petting?"

Good grief, I don't know how this woman's mind works, Miranda thought. She decided to be completely honest.

"We've kissed twice in our lives. And both times we agreed that we're too young for that sort of thing. We want to be just friends," Miranda said, wondering if the "agree" part was stretching the truth just a little.

"Chris said he just wanted to be friends? He agreed to that?" Was Mrs. Bergman reading her mind?

"He agreed to respect my wishes. Chris is one of my best friends, and I don't want anything to spoil that. So, yes, we agreed. No more kissing until we're older. He is a true gentleman. You must have taught him that."

Mrs. Bergman thought a long minute before she said, "Wait right here, please."

Miranda waited several minutes for Mrs. Bergman to come back. When she finally did, Chris was with her. A tingle of joy ran through Miranda at the sight of him. She wished she could hug him, but just smiled instead.

"I asked Chris some questions about what you told me and his answers proved that you're telling the truth," Mrs. Bergman said. "I'm sorry. I guess I did misjudge you both." She smiled. "Forgive me?"

"Yes, of course! Does this mean he can come over?"

"Now?"

"I'd like for him to come meet our visitors, but if he can't, we need to talk right here. We have an important decision to make."

"May I listen?" Mrs. Bergman asked.

"Sure. We'll want your approval." She turned to Chris. "I want to give Star to Teddy Hungry Horse."

"Give her away?" Chris asked in surprise. "Why, because she's sick?"

"Because he can make her well—*is* making her well."

"What do you mean?"

Miranda told him of the change that came over Shooting Star the minute Teddy arrived, how she'd been eating ever since, and how her energy had picked up. "Her whole attitude has changed, but if he leaves without her, she'll go back to the way she was."

"We don't know that, do we?"

"I think it's pretty obvious. Nothing you or I or anyone else did for her made a difference, but just seeing Teddy did. I don't want to lose her. It kills me to let her go, but she has chosen. I can't own her spirit or her love."

"Wait," Mrs. Bergman said. "Isn't this horse worth thousands of dollars? And you're thinking of just giving her away? If she is so much better with this Teddy, let him buy her."

"Mrs. Bergman, I can't do that. If you or if Chris want payment for his half, I'll find a way to pay it. But Teddy can't afford it. And they need to be together."

"Mom, as she is now, Shooting Star isn't worth a dime. She's skin and bones and will be dead in months unless we do something. If there is nothing we can do but watch her die, why should we get paid for her?"

"Well, we can discuss money matters later with your father. Run along. If the only way to save her is to send her home with this boy, do it."

Miranda introduced Chris to Lucille and Teddy. Together they held out the registration paper that both of them had signed. "We want you to take Star home with you. She has chosen you. She's yours," Miranda said.

Teddy's smile was worth all the heartache of losing a horse. His eyes filled with tears as he hugged first Miranda and then Chris, thanking them.

"But, we can't take your horse without paying for her," Lucille said.

"Oh, but Teddy has paid for her. Don't you see? He has saved my life three times. I happen to think my life is worth more than money. Please let him take her."

"Three times?"Lucille asked.

"When he found me in the snow, unconscious, and took me to the cave was the first one."

"Yes, and when he talked the man out of his gun," Lucille interjected.

"The other time was when he made me poultices and tea from juniper berries. The doctor said that I probably would have died of the infection if he hadn't done those things."

Lucille smiled and hugged Miranda. "I'm thankful for your life, and I agree it's worth more than any amount of money. Thank you for letting Teddy have your horse."

"His horse. Star convinced me that she is his. I may have had her papers, but he has her heart."

Lucille looked at the paper in her hand. "You know when we register her, Teddy might want to change her name. Will you be offended by that?"

"I guess not. But I don't understand why. I thought Shooting Star was the perfect name for the her."

"Teddy, why do you like 'Rising Sun' better than 'Shooting Star?'" his grandmother asked.

"She is the exact color of the sunrise the morning I found her."

"Is that all?" Miranda was prepared to argue the merits of the name, Shooting Star, for the marking on her forehead.

"No, that is not the only reason. It is also because the sun rises every day. It is faithful. But a shooting star is seen only one time, and then it is gone. She is faithful like the rising sun, not the shooting star."

"Oh, I see."

"Yes, and even though she may leave this world someday when she is very old, she will live forever in my heart. She is my Rising Sun."

"Okay," Miranda agreed. "Well, let's get her loaded."

Dad helped hitch the small trailer to Lucille's pickup, and Teddy led Rising Sun into the trailer. She followed him without hesitation.

Tears flowed down Miranda's cheeks as she watched them drive away.

Chris put his arm over her shoulder. "I know," is all he said. She pulled away and ran to the barn. She didn't want Chris or anyone else to see her cry. She felt the need to be alone. Alone with her very best friend, Starlight.

She took his bridle and went to his paddock. He came to meet her, as usual, and lowered his head. She placed her hand on his forehead and then leaned against him, hugging his beautiful head. She put his halter on, led him to the fence, climbed it, and slid onto his back.

She rode him bareback, loving the feel of his sleek coat and rippling muscles beneath her legs. She felt like she was an extension of him. He responded to her every movement, to the slightest tightening and easing of her muscles. She guided him along the river and up the mountainside to the top of Silver Butte. There, she laid her head against his neck and closed her eyes.

"At least I still have you, Starlight. I will never let you go to anyone, no matter how much they might love you and want you," she whispered. "No one could possibly love you more than I do. Of course, I thought that about Shooting Star, too. Or Rising Sun, that is. We'll miss her, but we have each other."

Miranda lost track of time. She let her mind wander as her tears dried up and the sun warmed her back. She dozed off and woke with a start when Starlight stiffened and his body vibrated with a low, welcoming nicker.

Miranda sat up and spotted the gleaming copper coat of a horse coming through the trees below. Her breath caught in her throat when for a split second she thought it was Star. A twinge of disappointment followed when she saw Queen, carrying Chris, emerge into the full sunlight.

They approached slowly, Chris's eyes never leaving her face. "I'll leave if you still want to be alone," he said when he was close enough for her to hear.

"No. That's okay," and she realized with surprise that she meant it. She didn't want him to go.

"You going to be okay?" he asked.

"Yes. I'll miss Star, but I still have Starlight, my other horses, and my friends." Miranda smiled and added, "Thanks for coming and finding me."

Chris had moved Queen alongside Starlight, facing the opposite direction until he was even with Miranda, their faces only a couple of feet apart. As she returned Chris's gaze, looking into his deep blue eyes, her heart skipped a beat and a lump rose in her throat. She felt like she was looking into a pool of clear water she'd like to jump into. She was sure she'd find his very soul if she could. *No*, she told herself, *I'm already looking into his soul, and it's honest, devoted, and loving*. *Limerence,* she thought as her breath caught in her throat. She remembered Laurie's words, *So what's wrong with that? Call it whatever you want, but it's love, and love is good."*

When she saw Chris's gaze move from her eyes to her lips she looked away, breaking the spell.

"Miranda," Chris began in a voice husky with emotion.

"I know. Don't say anything," Miranda interrupted. "You are about the best friend I have in the world. I love your honesty, your sense of humor, your eyes—oh my gosh, I love your eyes. I want us to be friends for life."

"Yeah, thanks, Miranda," Chris said in a flat, irony-filled voice.

"Please be patient with me, Chris. If it helps any, I can tell you I want to kiss you, but—I won't. Not yet."

Chris looked at her helplessly, shaking his head to show he didn't understand her reluctance. She wasn't sure she did either. But it seemed important.

"It's because I care about you—about us," she said.

Chris frowned.

Miranda shrugged and asked, "Friends?"

He sighed and smiled. "Friends," he said.

"All right!" Miranda said, laughing. She looked over her shoulder and pointed with her chin. "I'll race you to the lone tree at the end of the butte. Loser gets to muck out the barn."

Chris raised his reins, clapped his legs against Queen's side, and they were off like a shot before Miranda could turn Starlight around. She dropped the halter rope and leaned over Starlight's neck to retrieve it. He lunged forward, stepped on the rein, and nearly unseated Miranda when he stopped abruptly.

Clinging to his neck, she finally managed to right herself, gain her balance, and urge him forward. When she reached the tree, Chris sat relaxed on Queen.

"What took you so long?" he asked, a huge smile lighting his face.

"Well, it wasn't exactly an even start."

"Don't worry, I'll help you muck the barn."

"Thanks," she said, grinning. "I would've helped if I had won, too."

"I know. We're friends, right?"

"You bet. Forever."

"Miranda. You know that couples can be friends, don't you?"

"Well, I'd hope so." She laughed until she noticed that Chris looked a little worried, so she thought about his question.

"Mom and Dad say they are each other's best friends. I guess that's how marriage should be." Miranda said.

Chris grinned. "Then maybe when we are really, really old you'll let me kiss you—and we will still be friends."

Miranda opened her mouth to retort, but nothing came out. At last she smiled. "Well, yes, I think that's a very strong possibility."

Epilogue

Miranda saw Teddy only once the rest of that school year. He came with his grandmother to bring back the horse trailer they'd borrowed to take Shooting Star home. Their visit was short, arriving late afternoon, staying for supper, and spending the night, but rising before Miranda was even awake the next morning to head home. Teddy was so anxious to be with his horse.

Miranda threw herself into a rigorous schedule of working with the horses she had left. She still did her school work and choir, though she would have dropped it if her parents had let her. The work didn't keep her from thinking of Shooting Star and missing her, but it was her thoughts of Shooting Star that prompted her to work hard with every horse. There was always the thought in her mind that if only she'd spent more time with Star, maybe..., but she stopped the thought before she finished the "if only." Star had chosen Teddy. That was final. Let the other horses choose her.

It seemed especially imperative to spend a lot of time on Ebony who would soon be three years old and ready for the racing circuit. In late January, Shadow gave birth to Starlight's son. There was no white on him.

She didn't see Teddy over spring break, either. Both were too busy with their horses to even want to meet.

"I know how much you miss Shooting Star, and I miss her, too," Chris said to Miranda one warm day in April, "so, I've been thinking. Why don't we get a replacement for her."

"What are you talking about?"

"Queen's in heat right now. Let's put her in with Starlight."

Miranda's eyes widened and a smile turned into a giggle. "Yes, let's do it. We'll have Star's little sister bouncing around in our stable by this time next year."

"Or brother."

Miranda nodded, tied Ebony to the hitching rail in front of the barn, and walked with Chris and Queen to Starlight's paddock. They leaned on the fence watching the horses through the rails.

"What are you two up to now?" Dad asked as he walked around the corner from the barn. "Hey, I thought we had an agreement. No more foals until you got rid of some of your other horses."

"But we did. We gave Shooting Star away. This will be her replacement," Miranda said.

"Miranda, it seems to me that you have forgotten the basic concept of horse ranching."

"What concept?"

"For a ranch of any kind to succeed, it has to make money. Where is your income to pay for your horses' feed, vet bills, and the farriers, not to mention hay and pasture."

But we have plenty of pasture, and we put up hay from this place and the Caruthers place, so we don't have to buy any." Miranda stared at Dad, afraid of where this conversation was going.

"And who pays the mortgage on the Caruthers place, the taxes on both places, and the farm equipment and repair and fuel bills to do all that?"

"Well, I suppose you and Grandpa do that."

"And you think that's fair?"

"Well, no, but I give you the money that Chris and Laurie pay for boarding their horses."

"Yes, and that's a drop in the bucket compared to the expenses your horses incur."

"You and mom have the calves you raise and sell."

"Yes, we do. And you think that money should go to keeping your horses?"

Miranda glared at Dad, then she looked at her feet, but said nothing.

"How do you think Mr. Taylor funded Shady Hills?"

Miranda jerked her head up to meet his eyes. "With money he won racing his horses. If you'd let me enter more races, I'd give you all the prize money."

"He made very little money racing horses. There is a big entry fee to those races, so just entering is a gamble," Dad said. "He entered them mainly to show them, to market the horses he wanted to sell and the stud services he charged a huge price for."

"I don't want to make money off Starlight that way. If there are a lot of mares to be bred, it takes a lot out of a horse. You saw how thin Mr. Taylor's Knight would get. And how can you ask me to sell my horses? Isn't that just like asking you to sell your children?"

"No, it's not. You said you always wanted a horse ranch. If that's true, it's time you started making it pay."

When Dad walked away, Miranda's once jubilant mood had turned dark and brooding. She turned back to the fence.

"Well, at least we'll have a replacement for Star," Chris said.

The rest of the school year passed quickly with no more talk about Miranda selling her horses or stud services. But she knew it was coming. Dad and Miranda with two horses, Starlight and Ebony, were on their way to the Crow Fair in August when Dad brought it up.

"Miranda, it's time you made a decision. By the time we get back home, I want you to have made a choice. Either you grow up and become a responsible business owner, or you remain a child—which you are, by the way—and choose one horse for a pet and sell the rest."

Tears clouded Miranda's eyes and she was unable to speak for a moment. But she knew Dad was right. "I don't have to wait to decide. I'll be a horse rancher, but I'll need your help to make the right decisions." She took a deep ragged breath and continued. "It won't be easy, though. I love every one of my horses."

"I know," Dad said. "And I'll help you." He patted her knee and turned his eyes back to the road, but not before Miranda saw them sparkle with unshed tears.

When they drove into the encampment at Crow Agency, they spotted Teddy right away. Miranda thought he must have been watching for them. He smiled broadly and told them he would show them where they could put there horses—in with Rising Sun. He seemed different, somehow, Miranda thought. For one thing, he'd grown taller since he and Lucille had come to visit. But it was more than that. He seemed more confident, more outgoing. She decided he was just happy with his life, happy with who he was.

When the horses were unloaded and had greeted Rising Sun as horses do, Teddy went with them to sign up for the events they would enter. Dad, with his Cherokee certification, and Miranda, with the board's approval, would enter races and take part in the parades and dances.

Miranda and Teddy staged an unofficial race between Rising Sun and her sire, Starlight. The race was so close that no one was sure which horse had come in first. They tried again with Rising Sun winning by a nose. The next time, Starlight won.

"You should enter her in some big races, Teddy," Miranda said, "I know she'd win. She's in fine shape and obviously ready if she can beat Starlight." It was true. Rising Sun was as healthy as she'd ever been.

Teddy shook his head. "No. I will ride her in some races here, but I will never take her to big national ones."

"Why not? There's big prize money for those races, not to mention the fame. The whole world would be talking about her."

"I don't want those things for her. She is my soul mate and friend, not someone to make me rich or famous. I will not put her in that kind of danger."

"What danger?"

The danger caused by fame, greed, and jealousy. Stuff like that. I don't want her so famous that someone would want to take her from me. I don't want her to be competition for someone who would harm her just so he could win."

Miranda nodded. She couldn't argue with him. She'd seen such things happen when she was on the racing circuit with Mr. Taylor.

She smiled. "You're right, of course. And I see that Shooting Star—I mean, Rising Sun—chose wisely."

Miranda wiped tears from her eyes. She couldn't tell if they were tears of joy or sorrow. She thought she would always miss her Star, but she guessed her happiness for Teddy and Rising Sun was greater than the sadness she'd been feeling for her loss.

"Why is it you seem so wise for your age?" she asked, smiling at Teddy. Sobering, she asked a question that had been bothering her. "I read Chief Plenty Coups's biography. He was a very brave and wise man, but how can you follow in his footsteps? I mean, times have changed. You can't count coup in the same way he did, can you?" She thought of stories she'd read about the wars between tribes—scalp taking, horse stealing, and the killing as they fought over land that was gradually shrinking as the white man took more for himself.

Teddy frowned. "Of course not. The great chief saw the future and told us exactly how the times would change. He was right, and he gave us a new way to live and hold on to our land. He told us to keep our tradition, but to educate ourselves so that we could know all that the white man knows. So we count coup and earn feathers for our warbonnets in different ways. Some have done it by getting a college degree, some by serving in the US military. He told us to go to the white man's schools, to learn what the white man knows. He said they are here to stay and we must learn with them, but to bring our knowledge home to help our own people. I will not forsake the old ways that make me Apsáalooke. I cleanse myself in the sweat lodges. I seek wisdom in visions and dreams as I did in the Pryor Mountains. Just like our last great chief, I aim to be chief someday."

"But the Crows don't have a chief anymore."

"No, but the United States does."

Miranda opened her eyes wide in surprise. "You want to be president?"

"Do you think that is impossible?"

"No," Miranda said, laughing. "Nothing is impossible for you, if you believe in it. You have my vote, that's for sure."

Teddy grinned in a way that made Miranda think he knew something that she didn't. And he probably did.

The End

Acknowledgments

To the many young readers who asked me to write a seventh *Miranda and Starlight* book, thank you. It took several years for you to convince me that there was more to tell, and now I am glad you did.

To the many friends, editors, and authors who, at some point in the process, read, edited, and proofread the manuscript, I appreciate your suggestions and encouragement. If any mistakes remain after all your help, it is because I kept changing things, and I accept full responsibility for any errors.

I wish to express undying gratitude to two very special friends: Raven Publishing's late editor, Florence Ore, who helped with early drafts of this book and, as she has always done, gave good advice and direction, and to author Marcia Melton, who patiently and meticulously read draft after draft and helped improve the content of each rewrite.

Thanks to Rabbit Knows Gun, who taught me some of the Crow word I use in the book. I am especially grateful to Vivian Winter Chaser, Lakota, for pointing out things that might offend Native People. I hope that nothing remains that may be construed as disrespect, for I have the highest regard for not only the Crow people, but also other First Nations.

Special thanks, too, to the talented artist, Pat Lehmkuhl, who created the image for this book's cover as she has done for all of the previous *Miranda and Starlight* books.

Resource Guide

For More information about Crow Culture and other things found in this book.

http://www.bigorrin.org/crow_kids.htm — for a "Crow Indian Fact Sheet" by Laura Redish and Orrin Lewis whose site is *Native Languages of the Americas.* From there, find many links to other sites and books for a wealth of information

http://en.wikipedia.org/wiki/Crow_Nation — A good overview of the culture and history, with links to other sites.

http://native-american-indian-facts.com/Great-Plains-American-Indian-Facts/Crow-Indian-Facts.shtml

http://serc.carleton.edu/research_education/nativelands/crow/culture.html

http://stateparks.mt.gov/chief-plenty-coups/ — The Chief Plenty Coups State Park is fun and a great resource.

http://lib.lbhc.edu/index.php?q=node/71 — a biography of Chief Plenty Coups

http://biography.yourdictionary.com/plenty-coups

Plenty-Coups: Chief of the Crows (Bison Books) - November 1, 2002 by Frank Linderman *http://en.wikipedia.org/wiki/Little_People_of_the_Pryor_Mountains* — Awakkulé: Ferocious or helping or both?

http://www.pryormountains.org/welcome-to-the-pryors/why-are-the-pryors-special/

http://en.wikipedia.org/wiki/War_bonnet — Warbonnets are earned and respected.

http://myculturеisnotatrend.tumblr.com/post/774173677/war-bonnet-appropriation-etiquette-dont-do-it

http://lib.lbhc.edu/index.php?q=node/161 — Important curriculum guidelines for teaching Apsaalooké tradition and culture in schools. "Maybe if we learned more about each other all of Montana's diverse communities would appreciate, rather than demean their individuality."

https://nc-cherokee.com/ Official site of the Eastern Band of the Cherokee Nation

Many more sources are available for information about all Native American tribes through Internet searches.